The Girlfriend Project

The Girlfriend Project

Robin Friedman

Walker & Company
New York

First published in the United States of America in 2007 by Walker Publishing Company, Inc.
Paperback edition published in 2008
Distributed to the trade by Macmillan

For information about permission to reproduce selections from this book, write to
Permissions, Walker & Company, 175 Fifth Avenue, New York, New York 10010

The Library of Congress has cataloged the hardcover edition as follows:
Friedman, Robin.
The Girlfriend Project / Robin Friedman.
p.   cm.
Summary: New Jersey high school senior Reed Walton has never had a girlfriend,
but once he gets his braces off, gets contact lenses, and turns into a "hottie,"
his two best friends set up a Web site to remedy the situation.
ISBN-13: 978-0-8027-9624-0 • ISBN-10: 0-8027-9624-9 (hardcover)
[1. Identity—Fiction. 2. Dating (Social customs)—Fiction. 3. High schools—Fiction.
4. Schools—Fiction. 5. Web sites—Fiction. 6. New Jersey—Fiction.]   I. Title.
PZ7.F89785 Gi 2007   [Fic]—dc22   2006016088

ISBN-13: 978-0-8027-9781-0 • ISBN-10: 0-8027-9781-4 (paperback)

Visit Walker & Company's Web site at www.walkeryoungreaders.com

Book design by Donna Mark
Typeset by Westchester Book Composition
Printed in the U.S.A. by Quebecor World Fairfield
2 4 6 8 10 9 7 5 3 1

All papers used by Walker & Company are natural, recyclable products
made from wood grown in well-managed forests. The manufacturing processes
conform to the environmental regulations of the country of origin.

For my adorable brother,
Jonathan Ben-Joseph,
an Ultimate Nice Guy.

The Girlfriend Project

Who You Lookin' At?

Exit 1

My name is Reed Walton, I'm seventeen years old, I live in New Jersey, and I've never had a girlfriend.

Yeah. That's pretty much it.

Well, actually, no.

I've never kissed a girl either.

Pathetic? Sure. Don't you think I know that? I mean, at this rate, I'm headed for the priesthood.

But my best friends, Ronnie and Lonnie White, have decided Things Will Drastically Change when senior year officially starts tomorrow.

See, they've signed me up for something they're calling . . . *The Girlfriend Project*.

I'm in big, big trouble.

I know it's my last hope. But I don't have to like it.

It happens like this . . .

We're in my car—a Range Rover the color of swamp water—and we're parked in front of the Woodrow Wilson Basketball Courts at the George Washington Municipal Park. I don't know what these two presidents have to do with sports or trees, but this is New Jersey, like I said. George Washington slept here, and Woodrow Wilson was our governor, and I guess when you're New Jersey, you have to take what you can get.

A girl—a really cute girl—is shooting baskets by herself. I've been watching her since we got here. I'm doing a better job at this than listening to my friends' plans for getting me a girlfriend.

"So, Reed, whaddaya think?" Lonnie asks me, leaning forward from the backseat. I can smell his cologne when he's this close, and I wonder, Should I wear cologne? Is that the secret?

"I think not," I reply automatically.

"You're making a mistake," Ronnie says from the front seat. I trust her opinion more. After all, she's a girl, Lonnie's fraternal-twin sister. But she's siding with him on this one.

"I don't want a girlfriend," I lie through my teeth, knowing it'll never fly.

"You want a girlfriend so bad I can smell it," Ronnie replies, and sniffs the air loudly to make her point.

Maybe I *should* wear cologne. I feel self-conscious all of a sudden.

"I don't want to make a big deal out of it," I say. "Besides, I can take care of it."

"Yeah?" Lonnie says, and I hear a big-scary challenge coming.

"See that girl?" He points, but he doesn't have to. I haven't taken my eyes off her. "Ask her out, buddy."

My stomach plunges eighteen stories, and I do the only thing I can think of—stall. "What—um—right now—right this very minute—just like that?"

Lonnie folds his arms across his chest. "Right now. Right this very minute. Just like that."

I gulp loudly. "But . . . It's just . . . You can't . . . What about . . . ?"

Ronnie pokes me playfully in the ribs. "You, cowboy, need *The Girlfriend Project.*"

They're right. I need *The Girlfriend Project* so bad *I* can smell it.

We're in my room making plans later that afternoon—the day before senior year starts at Marlborough Regional High School. Ronnie, who has a neon pink clipboard propped on her knees, is definitely working hard on it. Lonnie, on the other hand, just wants to pig out. She watches him in disgust as he stuffs three brownies into his mouth in rapid-fire succession.

"What?" he asks with his mouth full of chewed-up brownie. "You got a problem?"

"Boys," she mutters. "They never have to count calories, carbs, or fat grams."

Lonnie nods. "We're genetically superior."

"You're genetically mutated," Ronnie counters, then turns to me. "Anyway, Reed, back to you. How tall are you now?"

"Six foot one," I answer. I know this exactly, because I've been diligently measuring my height all summer.

Ronnie smiles at me. "Girls dig tall guys."

Lonnie nods again. "The girl's right."

Well, Lonnie ought to know. He's six foot three and has always had plenty of girls around.

Ronnie studies me. I think she's looking at my hair.

"Sandy," she murmurs.

Lonnie stops chewing and looks at her. "Who's Sandy?"

"His hair," Ronnie replies.

This response doesn't help very much.

Ronnie sighs. "His hair is sandy, you know, the color of sand."

Now Lonnie looks indignant. "The color of *sand*?!"

"It's dirty-blond, okay?" she sputters.

I nervously run my fingers through my sandy, dirty-blond hair, wishing Ronnie would stop staring at me. But what she does next makes me blush.

"Eye color," she says, and propels herself into my face.

I try not to blink or move as she gazes deeply into my eyes, but I can feel my cheeks flame.

How will I go on dates with girls when just having my best friend's face near mine makes my whole neck go on fire?

I'm more hopeless than I thought.

"Brown," Lonnie says definitively from across the room. He leans toward me, and for one panic-stricken second, I think he's going to get in my face too, which would be a real low point. But he just hands me the empty plate of brownies. "The color of brownies. Refill, Reed."

I take the plate and start to get up.

"No," Ronnie says, and I'm not sure if she's talking about my eyes or the brownies. "More like hazel." She scribbles. "I'm so glad you finally got rid of the glasses, Reed, you have nice eyes. Girls dig nice eyes."

"The girl's right."

Ronnie ignores him. "Honey," she says.

"Who's Honey?"

Ronnie throws her brother another murderous look, then peers at me in a dreamy sort of way. "Like a jar of honey on a kitchen shelf when the sun shines through it. That's the color of your eyes."

We look at her blankly.

"Boys," she mutters. "Neanderthals with no imagination."

Actually, I was trying to picture that sun-drenched jar of honey. Maybe I'll examine my eyes more closely later to see if it's true. I can't believe having eyes the color of honey is going to matter with girls one way or the other, but I'm not going to argue with the experts.

"Be right back," I say, indicating the empty plate.

I hope they don't strangle each other while I'm gone, but you never know. I head down the stairs to the kitchen. My house is one of those just-out-of-the-oven-homemade-cookies-cakes-and-brownies kind of house. That's because my grandmother lives with my parents and me. She loves baking.

Ronnie and Lonnie—yup, those are their real names—have always lived next door to us, and the three of us have been best friends since kindergarten. And get this, their parents are

Bonnie and Donnie White. And their cats are Connie and Johnnie. How can you not love a family like that?

When I walk into the kitchen, I hear my grandmother making huffing-and-puffing noises as she reaches into a high cabinet for something.

"I'll get that for you, Grandma," I say.

She pinches my cheek as I retrieve a bag of flour for her.

"You're a good boy, Reed," she says.

Yup, good boy, that's me.

All-Around Nice Guy. Average Joe. All-American Boy Next Door.

Most Likely Not to Offend Anyone. Most Likely to Blend into the Wallpaper.

Dorkus Extremus.

The kind of guy who babysits his nieces and nephews, sets the table for dinner every night, and blushes in an *aw-shucks* way when Grandma tells her blue-haired old-lady friends I'm a straight-A student shooting for Princeton.

I'm even an Eagle Scout. Scout's honor! Ha ha ha.

But things may finally change for me. See, over the summer, I got my braces taken off, grew another inch or two, started wearing contact lenses, and got a car.

Ronnie says girls dig tall guys with nice eyes, a nice smile, and a car.

The Girlfriend Project—here we go.

Ready or not.

I Got Your $%#& State Motto Right Here!

Exit 2

I get the first hint that Things are Completely Different Now when I stop at my locker the next morning. Rhonda Wharton is there, at the locker next to mine, in a short black dress that hits me like an eighteen wheeler. I try not to be obvious about it, but it's hard. Rhonda is so hot that part of my brain is melting.

The first day of school is always a blur to me, what with everyone catching up, showing off their not-from-the-tanning-salon tans, running all over trying to find new classes, getting used to a brand-new schedule. I've got a full load of AP classes again this year, and the folks at the Ivy League will probably want to see my final transcript. Not that I'm worried about it. I'm worried about other things.

I open my locker and start the day's Shifting Around of Heavy Textbooks. But what I'm really thinking about is how

I can compliment Rhonda on her dress without coming off like a perv. It would be a nice way to open *The Girlfriend Project*. Ronnie would be proud.

Rhonda and I have been next-door locker neighbors since middle school. We're seated next to each other in every class the teacher arranges students by alphabetical order. We're not friends, exactly, more like alphabet acquaintances. If not for the location of our lockers, a girl like Rhonda wouldn't know I breathed the same air she did. As I'm pondering this, Rhonda turns to me, I smile, and she does a double take.

"Reed?" she whispers, her big brown eyes as wide as a doe's. "What . . . You're . . . Is that really you?"

I'm not sure whether to be flattered or insulted by her reaction. Those were very thick Coke-bottle glasses I used to wear, and I had those braces for so long it shocked me, too, that actual teeth were under them. I'm kind of surprised by their whiteness and straightness. I guess braces really work.

"Hi, Rhonda," I say, as if nothing's different. "How was your summer?"

She wants to answer—her mouth moves—but no words come out. I realize it's the effect I've always had on girls. Even now, being new and improved, they're not talking to me.

I take a deep breath. "That's a . . . totally cool dress."

Totally cool? *Argh.* That's the best I can do?

But Rhonda smiles at me. "You like it?"

This throws me off. Didn't I just tell her I did?

"Um, yeah," I reply. "Totally cool."

Argh!—not again. I don't seem to have trouble with vocabulary when I'm writing essays for AP English. Why does that part of my brain cortex die when I'm around girls?

Rhonda continues to smile, and I can't help thinking I should do something. But what? The way she's looking at me . . .

"You're, like, a completely different person, Reed," she says. Her cheeks are pink. Is she blushing? Because of *me*? "I didn't know you could be so . . . cute."

Cute?

Me?

Me?

I swallow hard. I'm *definitely* supposed to do something. I can feel it. It's in the air around us. But I don't know what it is. I can't decode it. My brain is all fogged up, frozen, useless. Rhonda Wharton, with her big brown eyes and short black dress, is smiling at me, waiting for me to do the thing I'm supposed to do, and all I can come up with is this: "Better hurry— homeroom bell's gonna ring soon."

The smile melts off her face. Melts. Just like that. Like an ice-cream cone, a beautiful, perfectly formed chocolate ice-cream cone, flattening into an ugly brown puddle. She turns away from me.

I've screwed up big-time. I wasn't supposed to say that. That much I know. But it's too late to fix it. Even if I knew *how* to fix it.

Rhonda slams her locker shut, mumbles something to me, and takes off.

I curse my new and improved self.

. . .

"You were supposed to ask her out," Lonnie informs me at lunch. We're in the school cafeteria a few hours later.

"What—just like that?" I can't get the hang of this spontaneous-asking-out thing. Maybe I'm missing the right gene. It would explain a lot.

I haven't touched my orange-colored sloppy Joe or soggy French fries. All morning, my stomach has been twisted up in a tangled knot. All I see is Rhonda Wharton stomping away from me, and all I hear is the angry slam of her locker.

"Yeah, just like that, Romeo," Lonnie replies nonchalantly, tipping back his head and pouring a can of Mountain Dew into his mouth.

I stab my food with a plastic fork that's missing one of its tines. I wonder if it broke off inside the mysterious contents of the sloppy Joe I'm not eating.

"He's right, Reed," Ronnie says softly. I can tell from her tone she's feeling sorry for me. They're both sitting across from me, looking at me like I'm some kind of charity case, which I guess I am.

The noise level in the cafeteria is super-high. We're over by the floor-to-ceiling windows at a brand-new table this year. The tables by the windows are the best ones, reserved for the senior class, not officially, but in an unspoken-code kind of way. I can't believe I've finally managed to make it here. So, why do I feel like I'm back in ninth grade?

"But . . . ," I begin, gazing at my best friends, but I honestly don't know where to begin. Where is this stuff written down? Where do I buy the textbook? How was I supposed to know I should've asked Rhonda out? Besides, what if she said no? I say this part out loud.

"She *wanted* you to ask her out," Ronnie says. "She wouldn't have said no."

"How do you know that?" I ask cluelessly.

"Because it's obvious, Reed."

"How?"

She sighs, reaches over, and musses up my hair. "You have a brain that can solve calculus problems, write essays about lost civilizations, and memorize poetry, but when it comes to girls, it turns into mush."

Yeah—that pretty much sums it up.

"I'm a lost cause," I mumble, and I mean it.

"You just need some help. That's what *The Girlfriend Project* is all about."

"I need a class—with a syllabus and homework assignments."

Ronnie leans forward. "Life's not a class, Reed. You can't learn everything from textbooks. You have to *experience* it. You have to get back on the horse."

"Horse?" I ask in confusion. "Does this mean I have to ask Rhonda out?"

Lonnie shakes his head and looks at me with pity. "It's too late for that, buddy."

"Too late?"

"You pissed her off," he says matter-of-factly.

"I did?" This is astonishing to me. "But I didn't do anything!"

"Exactly."

"So . . . ," I say, and immediately hate the whine in my voice. "That's it?"

"That's it," he informs me. "For now."

"But this is crazy!" I exclaim, throwing up my hands. "It makes no sense. You're making it sound like she hates me."

"She does hate you. In a way." This astounding, news-to-me statement comes from Ronnie.

"But I didn't do anything!" I say again, feeling very much like the four walls of the noisy school cafeteria are closing in on me. If this is the way girls and dating are supposed to work, I don't see how I'll ever get it. It doesn't matter how tall I am, or how much my teeth sparkle, or how nice my eyes are.

Ronnie shakes her head, as if she's trying to explain something very simple to a total ignoramus. Which is *precisely* what's going on here. "I didn't realize how much help you need, Reed, I thought it would be enough that you look different. But, you know, you don't *feel* different. Not yet anyway. This is going to take lots of hard work."

Ah, the magic words. "I'm not afraid of hard work."

"That's the spirit." A sly expression crosses her face. "Forget Rhonda Wharton. You've got bigger fish to fry."

I try to make the image of Rhonda's long legs and short dress leave my mind before what Ronnie just said sinks in.

"You mean . . . ," I croak.

Ronnie nods. "Marsha Peterman's locker. Last bell."

I actually slump in my chair. "No," I whisper. "She shot me down last time."

"That was four years ago," Ronnie says. "And you've been pining for her ever since. Hasn't the time come? Come on, Reed, it's not Chinese torture."

"It is too."

She looks annoyed. "Why do boys make such a humongous deal out of asking girls out? I thought you were supposed to be tough guys."

"We're not tough guys," I mumble.

"Hey, speak for yourself, son," Lonnie says, but I know he's just kidding. Lonnie may have a smooth, pretend-tough exterior, but like most of us guys, his ego's softer than Marshmallow Fluff.

"It's like you're crybabies or something," Ronnie goes on.

Ronnie, on the other hand, is definitely blunt, but that's a good thing. She's the kind of person who tells you when you have lettuce stuck in your teeth.

"We're not crybabies," I say quietly.

Ronnie must sense she's hit a raw nerve because she says, "I'm sorry I said that, Reed. I know you're trying. I didn't mean it."

I want to keep talking about it, but Lonnie's Chick Clique has officially begun. They giggle up to our table to catch up with him.

I get up before anyone has a chance to notice the new

and improved me. I've had enough of the new and improved me.

"Where are you going, Reed?" Ronnie asks me.

"The library."

"But, Reed, your destiny awaits you."

"My destiny is with my AP Spanish textbook, Ronnie. *Adios, amigos.*"

. . .

The pity party goes on all day.

I try to concentrate on classes, but I can't. What Ronnie said to me won't go away.

People continue to comment on the new and improved me, and girls who have never given me the time of day seem suddenly friendly. I'm too rattled to pay attention.

Why have I always been so uncomfortable around girls?

Because I'm shy? Or because of Ronnie and Lonnie?

When your best friends have always lived next door to you, why should you get into the habit of making new friends, talking to people you don't know, or asking out girls?

I've never gone anywhere without one of them by my side, whether it's a party, the mall, the movies, or the school cafeteria. The thought of doing something by myself is terrifying to me. I guess my life up to now has been one long episode of *Fear Factor:*

Fear of being laughed at.

Fear of looking stupid.

Fear of failure.

Fear of being rejected.

Fear of bad breath.

Fear of saying the wrong thing.

Fear of being the wrong thing.

You should know, though, that while I'm definitely a dork, I'm not a nerd. There's a difference.

A nerd has a funny haircut, wears pants that are too short, has ballpoint pens in his shirt pocket, and gets picked on by other kids.

My hair and clothes are fine (thanks to Ronnie), I don't have ballpoint pens in my shirt pocket, and I've never been picked on by other kids (thanks to Lonnie).

I guess the three of us all started out at the same place way back in kindergarten, but somewhere around fifth grade, Ronnie and Lonnie diverged onto the popular path and I diverged onto the dork path. They have other friends besides me—the popular kids—but I'm the one they trust. That's what they always tell me, anyway. I'm lucky to have them. And I'm lucky that they're popular enough that they don't have to worry about losing points for being seen with a dork like me.

Maybe being good at school is easier than being good at girls. After all, there are teachers and textbooks and tests—a whole bureaucracy—to help you get there.

Or maybe it's more like I never had a chance.

Or maybe it's just that I never tried.

By the time the last bell rings, I'm exhausted. I take my

time getting to my locker, worried about running into Rhonda Wharton again. I realize I won't be able to avoid her forever. I can't believe it's the first day of school and I've already made an enemy of the person whose locker is right next to mine.

But when I reach my locker, she's nowhere in sight. The hallway's crowded with people slamming lockers. I quickly pull out my stuff and decide to book out of there. But Ronnie and Lonnie pounce on me before I can escape. See, their last name starts with *W* too, which means they're in the same locker neighborhood as me.

"Your destiny calls, Reed," Ronnie says, pulling me down the hall.

"Let me go," I say through clenched teeth.

"No, Reed," she growls back. "There's only one way to do this. Sink or swim."

"So you want me to drown?" I ask. "You want to kill me?"

She gives me a serious look. "I want you to ask out the love of your life. I give you . . . Marsha Peterman."

And with that, she shoves me forward, right into the maw of the beast.

. . .

I've had a crush on Marsha Peterman since freshman year. Not that I've done anything about it in four years.

No, you don't need to tell me it's pathetic.

No, you don't need to tell me *I'm* pathetic.

Yeah, thanks, I'm fully aware of the situation.

I look behind me, frowning when I spot Ronnie and Lonnie

behind a bend in the lockers. Spies, they are. I don't know if that's good or bad. On the one hand, they'll witness my final, full-fledged humiliation of the day. On the other hand, they'll be able to provide CPR when I have my heart attack.

Marsha Peterman, a complete vision in robin's egg blue that's stretched tight in all the right places, has finished loading her backpack when I stumble into her presence. She peers at me questioningly with big eyes the exact shade of her outfit.

"Reed?" she asks in amazement.

I honestly don't know how to respond to these public exclamations of astonishment. Should I be grateful that people are noticing I'm new and improved? Or should I be mortified that I dared show myself in public before today?

"Hey, Marsha," I manage, trying not to ogle.

She gives me the whole wow-you're-like-a-different-person thing. Then she smiles wider. And waits. Expectantly.

I gulp. Okay. This is it. That smile. That waiting. Just like Rhonda Wharton. Except now I know what I'm supposed to do. I'm supposed to ask her out. Could that really be it? Marsha Peterman wants *me* to ask her out? Why would she want to go out with me? She's a goddess. She was a goddess when I made the ridiculous mistake of asking her out four years ago. She shot me down quicker than a sniper. And yet, to this day, I still zone out about her and me.

It dawns on me that I'm not ready for this. I need a prepared statement. Something I can read off. I can't ad-lib this. Why didn't we take care of that? What kind of stupid *Girlfriend Project*

17

is this? Hurling me out here without the proper tools? It's like asking me to open a coconut with my bare hands.

"Coconut," I blurt out.

She looks spooked. Really, really spooked. Who can blame her? What kind of idiot says things like that?

"Do you like coconut?" I ask quickly, trying to recover.

She smiles!

"Yeah, I do, a lot," she says.

This might have worked if I let it alone. But no.

"That's great. I guess it could hurt a lot if you got bonked on the head with a coconut, but that's great. Great. Great."

She starts to dart her eyes around, like she's looking for the nearest exit.

I start to sweat. Now I have body odor to worry about too.

Think, I order myself. You've seen Lonnie do this a million times. How does he do it? What does he say? He makes it look so easy! I beg my brain cells to give me the right words, but all I'm getting is Shakespeare.

"*Romeo and Juliet*," I say.

How much worse than *coconut* is this going to get?

Marsha arches a perfectly shaped eyebrow. Then she smiles again. Could it be I've said the right thing?

"Yes," she breathes.

What's happening? What does this mean?

"Yeah, we're reading that in AP English this year," I drone. "After *Hamlet*, then *Othello*, then *Much Ado About Nothing* . . ."

The smile slides off.

Buzzer! Wrong answer, Reed!

Her posture is changing. Her shoulders are turning away from me.

Say it. Say it. Say it.

One sentence.

Will you go out with me?

It's not suave, romantic, or even logical, I mean, go out with me where and when? But, at least, it's a starting place. It's a better starting place than *coconut*.

"Marsha, um, will you . . . go . . . trout with me?"

She hesitates. "Trout?"

Did I say *trout*?

She gets a hurt look on her face. Like I've said something mean and nasty. Like I've just made fun of her.

"That isn't funny," she snaps.

She walks away.

I feel like someone's punched me in the gut.

. . .

"Trout? You said 'trout'?" Lonnie shakes his head.

I know he's holding back major cracking up. In Lonnie's world, this is the stuff of late-night talk shows.

We're in my Range Rover heading to IHOP after school. Lonnie claps my shoulder.

"Forget about it, dude. Besides, there's nothing a big stack of chocolate chip pancakes can't fix." He smacks his lips noisily.

But I barely hear him. "But why did it upset Marsha so much? What's so offensive about trout in the first place?"

Ronnie, in the backseat, leans forward. "It could be anything, Reed. Maybe Marsha's grandfather was a trout fisherman and he fell overboard during a storm at sea. Maybe Marsha's aunt died choking on a trout bone."

"Maybe when Marsha was in third grade," Lonnie chimes in soberly, "someone called her Trout Wench. Or Trout Lips."

"But this is crazy!" I yell for the second time that day, pointing out the obvious, I think. "How am I supposed to know all this?" I force myself to concentrate on Route 18, but it's nearly impossible. "And what about the *Romeo and Juliet* thing? Why was Marsha so into it at first—and what did I say to get her out of it?"

Ronnie plays with the hair at the back of my neck, giving me a colossal case of goose bumps. It momentarily takes my mind off Marsha Peterman, but not long enough, unfortunately.

"Maybe . . . Marsha thought you were going to act out the balcony scene," Ronnie says dreamily. "Maybe she thought you were going to tell her she was the sun."

Lonnie winks at me. "Quote some of those sonnets, dude, and you've got it made."

I'm speechless.

What on earth are they talking about?

Quote sonnets? Act out balcony scenes?

I need drama lessons to get a date?

"That can't be right," I mutter. "It's crazy. Crazy. Crazy. Crazy."

I feel like one of those people who talks to themselves.

I see myself in twenty years, wandering the streets of Jersey City in a ratty old coat filled with used Kleenex and reciting lines from Shakespeare . . .

But, soft! What light through yonder window breaks?
It is the east and Juliet is the sun!

Ronnie leans forward. "This *Girlfriend Project* isn't going well, is it?"

This sets me off completely. "Well, it's not really a *Girlfriend Project* at all, is it?" I ask, the sarcasm sounding sharp even to me. "As far as I can tell, all this brilliant project consists of is you guys throwing me to the lions to be soundly torn into bloody shreds."

I know I'm being hard on them, but I can't help it. I'm mad. I'm really mad. I can't remember the last time I had such a rotten day.

Lonnie stares ahead silently and Ronnie gets all quiet. I feel awful about what I've just said. They didn't deserve that at all.

But Ronnie says, "No, you're right, Reed. You need more. Like I said. You're starting at the beginning. You need the basics."

Yet this feels downright insulting.

I pull into IHOP's parking lot. What Ronnie's saying is *true*. But, still, why am I putting myself through this? I mean, I've done *fine* up to now. I've had success in school. I've had friends. I haven't had a girlfriend. So what? Look what happens when I try to change. Why bother? Why not go back to my old safe self? I can't get my braces back, but I can wear my Coke-bottle glasses again. Or I can stay the way I am now, but forget this trying-to-get-a-girlfriend business.

Is it really worth it?

We exit the car and Ronnie takes my hand. "We'll work on this, Reed, I promise."

I'm not sure how I feel about it, but I do feel terrible about yelling at her. "I'm sorry I bit your head off, Ronnie," I say sheepishly.

She smiles. "It's okay. I know this isn't easy for you. But the funny thing is . . . both Rhonda and Marsha *liked* you, Reed. They would've said yes to you if you hadn't . . ."

"Screwed it up?" I supply in as casual a way as I can.

She giggles.

Well, it's true. Only I could bring coconut and trout into a question that should've been simple.

We enter the pancake house, the hostess shows us to our favorite U-shaped booth in the back, and we all slide in one by one. Ronnie and Lonnie pick up their menus, but I drum my fingers on the table.

"There's still something, though," I say. "Even if Rhonda and Marsha did like me." Saying that out loud sounds positively bizarre. I mean, they're two of the hottest girls in class and . . . I'm Professor Dork D. Dork.

"Why now?" I continue, turning this thought over aloud. "I asked Marsha Peterman out when we were freshmen and . . . she squashed me like a stinkbug."

Ronnie looks up from her menu. "I think that's kind of

obvious, Reed. Don't you think you're a . . . better specimen now?"

That's all the provocation I need. "There are two things
wrong with that, Ronnie. First, I'm the same as I always was.
Second, if that's true, this is about . . . looks."

"And your point is?" Lonnie asks.

"I'm the same as I always was," I sputter. "I haven't changed."

"But you look different," Ronnie says.

"But I'm *not* different," I say.

I have no idea what I'm trying to argue, and it's hard
enough making sense of it at an IHOP. All I know is, Ronnie
and Lonnie have always gotten me, and I wish they would now.

"It's okay to change, Reed," Ronnie says softly.

"But I haven't changed. I'm still—"

"Don't say it," Ronnie says.

"A dork."

She sighs. "You're not a dork." She leans toward me. "You're
a hottie."

This comment makes my entire body burn from scalp to
big toes. Why am I so like that about this?

"Better get used to it, beautiful," Ronnie says, reading
my mind.

I make a snorting noise. "But, Ronnie, inside . . ."

Ronnie gazes right at me. "Inside, you were *always* beautiful, Reed."

I look away in embarrassment, but Ronnie's comment
makes me instantly think of Valentine's Day. Every year, the
junior and senior classes sell carnations-for-delivery in school,

and every year, Ronnie buys one for me. Next to the prom and Homecoming, receiving a carnation on Valentine's Day is the biggest event of the year. Not getting one immediately brands you a loser—even if you're a guy. But mine always says, "For my beautiful best friend."

It's funny. Thinking about it now makes me feel very weird, but I didn't feel that way when the carnations were delivered. I was grateful. I mean, who else was going to send me one?

Maybe my "outside" has changed to match my "inside"— at least according to Ronnie—but I don't know if I'm ready to share either with the world. Or maybe I'm not sure Ronnie's right—either way.

I feel suddenly exhausted. Ronnie, however, isn't finished. Her blue eyes are fiery—it's a look I recognize—it means she's only getting started. "Besides, Reed, what about you? Don't looks matter to *you*?"

"Well . . . yeah," I admit.

Lonnie dives in headfirst. "Dude, what's wrong with being a physical object of lust? It's never bothered me."

I clear my throat noisily. "I don't know. It seems . . . dishonest."

Ronnie stares at me. "Well, then, I guess contact lenses are dishonest. And push-up bras. And high heels. I guess we need to get rid of these things. Is that what you want, Reed?"

I come to the conclusion that I have no idea what I'm talking about. "No," I mumble. "But what if I get disfigured like . . . the Elephant Man?"

"You're being melodramatic."

"Maybe I'm not ready for this," I say, finally getting to the point.

Lonnie takes over. "Look, buddy, next year you're going to be on your own. You have to do this. For your sake. This is good for you. It's healthy."

"Yeah," Ronnie agrees. "Like yogurt."

They're right . . . and it scares me to death. But I mutter, "I don't eat yogurt. It has female hormones like estrogen in it. And it's all fine and good for the two of you. You guys have never been alone."

Lonnie wasn't going with anyone now, but practically every girl in school wanted him. He was *It*. He and Deena Winters had broken up last year, but she'd take him back in a heartbeat.

And Ronnie? She was one of the prettiest girls in class. And she'd been with Jonathan Morrow since the junior prom. And there were three boyfriends before him. The line for Ronnie stretched all the way from here to Katmandu. And there was no spot for me in it.

"Besides," I say, trying to sound like I couldn't care less. "Girls like bad boys."

"Now you're being difficult," Ronnie says.

"Floyd Flavin got arrested last year and now he's the most popular guy in school—total pimp," I say.

"Well," Ronnie says. "We like celebrities. Sometimes it's the fame factor."

"Nice guys finish last," I mutter.

"Not in your case, Reed, not if we can help it."

. . .

We covered so much ground at IHOP I'm tired just thinking about it—looks, fame, celebrity, bad boys, nice guys, trout. Yet none of it makes any sense to me, and I don't know if it ever will. When I get home, I'm happy to help Grandma set up her laptop on the kitchen table to take my mind off things.

My grandmother bought a laptop last year. "It's a new millennium and it's time for me to get an e-mail address," she declared.

Grandma's friends thought she was loony. For them, computers are alien artifacts left behind by Martians, which must be shunned at all costs. But Grandma said, "Balderdash, Reed. It's when you stop growing that you get in trouble."

Now Grandma belongs to a dozen Listservs—from growing tea roses to baking bread to cruising the Caribbean to square dancing. Sometimes I think she spends more time online than I do.

Grandma's latest interest is our state motto contest. See, last year, the New Jersey Division of Tourism decided to update New Jersey's old motto, "New Jersey and You: Perfect Together." They hired a consultant from New York for $260,000 and got "New Jersey: We'll Win You Over."

Everybody hated that, naturally. I mean, yeah, we know it's our job to entertain the rest of the country, and yeah, we take it seriously. But maybe you better let us do the thinking—you might hurt yourself, you know? Besides, the new motto cost too much. And why go and hire a consultant from the state that's our natural nemesis? So, Acting Governor Richard Codey scrapped the bad motto and did what he should've done all along—invited regular New Jerseyans to submit suggestions online.

"New Jersey," Grandma says as she slides in front of her laptop, starting it off, as she always does, in the private contest between her and me, "More Than Just the Turnpike."

"New Jersey," I reply on cue, "At Least We're Not Delaware."

"New Jersey," Grandma retorts, "We Have Farms Too."

"New Jersey," I finish up, "Turn Signals Are for Wimps."

Grandma lets out a laugh. "Oh, that's a good one," she says, and begins typing. "I may have to share credit with you!" She turns to look at me. "My goodness, Reed, is there anything you're not good at?"

I stiffen, but cover it up. "I can't speak Mongolian to save my life."

Grandma laughs again. "Reed, you are precious."

Precious.

It beats loser, I guess.

When Grandma's done working on her laptop, I help her set the table for dinner like I do every night.

"New Jersey," she says as she lays down silverware, "The Beach, the Boss, the Best."

"New Jersey," I reply as I set down plates, "Come Here and Spend Money or We'll Break Your Legs."

Dad sweeps into the kitchen, carrying a stack of books and looking lost.

"Has anyone seen my reading glasses?" he asks.

"I see them on your head," I say.

Dad reaches one hand up and pulls his glasses over his face. "The old noggin's getting rusty," he says with a sigh. "Isn't what it used to be, my boy, isn't as young and sharp as yours."

"Well, naturally," I say. "It takes an absolute genius to spot glasses on top of someone's head."

Mom comes in and kisses my cheek. "How was your first day of school, hon?"

"Fine," I say with a shrug, setting down Grandma's beef brisket with mashed potatoes. I definitely don't want to get into any of it.

Mom takes her seat. "I'm sure you'll do great like you always do." She smiles at me. "You're our problem-free, hassle-free, no-maintenance kid."

Dad nods, bringing the peas to the table and taking his seat next to Mom. "Your mother's right. You practically raised yourself, you know."

"Nah, you guys just got lazy after Christine." I help my grandmother into her chair and take my seat.

They laugh. "Well, she was a terror compared to you," Mom says.

I feel more pathetic than usual. My older sister was the kind of teenage nightmare responsible for parental ulcers—stumbling home after curfew, partying, throwing temper tantrums, smashing vases against walls, yelling, screaming, providing nonstop drama.

The worst thing I ever did was spill red grape juice on my pants on Picture Day in seventh grade.

"Speaking of Christine, she needs your babysitting services this Saturday night," Mom says as we dig into Grandma's dinner.

Attention! Loser Alert!

I don't mind babysitting my nieces and nephews. But my parents assuming they have a standing right to impose on my Saturday nights shows just how pathetic I really am.

"Okay," I mumble, then wonder why they don't ask Grandma instead.

"Leo asked me to the Moon River Dance this Saturday night at the Moose Lodge," Grandma says, providing the answer.

Mom and Dad beam at her.

Ouch. My eighty-two-year-old grandmother has a hot date and I don't.

Grandma turns to me. "New Jersey," she says, "A Nice Place to Visit, But You Can't Afford to Live Here."

My heart's not in it, but I manage: "New Jersey: You Got a Problem with That?"

Everybody laughs, but I'm quiet for the rest of dinner. I go up to my room afterward and sit on my bed with my laptop. I get a message from Lonnie.

StudMonkey: need reedmobile 4 sat nite. ok?

It's beyond ironic that a dork like me has a car while a player like Lonnie doesn't. Usually he uses the family Camry. I type a message back.

ScreamingEagle: np. i'll be in loserville, USA, anyway. m/b i shud hand over the keys 4 gud.
StudMonkey: baby sitting duty?
ScreamingEagle: ya.
StudMonkey: bummer. next sat nite.
ScreamingEagle: wut?
StudMonkey: w8 & c.

I get a message from Ronnie.

FaerieCharmer: i'm working on *The Girlfriend Project* & it will be SWELL! L8r!

I laugh out loud. Ronnie's on a campaign to bring back words from the past. She's had enough of "cool."

ScreamingEagle: GROOVY.

I log off, wondering what my friends are up to. I feel crappy, for sure, relying on them for a love life. But I'm also grateful. A guy can't be a certifiable dweeb when he has friends like that.

Right?

Bada Bing, Bada Boom!

Exit 3

Rhonda Wharton is at her locker Friday morning, and this time she's wearing tight jeans that accentuate every luscious curve.

I pretend not to notice. She flings open her locker right into my forehead.

"Argh!" I yelp.

Did she do that on purpose?

"Oh, Reed, I'm sorry!" she cries, but she doesn't look very sorry.

"It's okay," I reply, rubbing the spot. "At least I'm awake now."

The corners of her mouth turn up slightly. She's holding back a smile.

I want to say something to her, but I don't know what. I'm too afraid of letting loose another stream of consciousness involving coconut and trout—and who knows what other fish and tropical fruit.

I see Marsha Peterman in the hall later that day too, but she ignores me completely.

Do I need this aggravation?

On the other hand, do I want to spend the rest of my senior year babysitting my nieces and nephews every Saturday night?

Being scared all the time is pretty exhausting. But it beats the alternative.

Or does it?

I mean, Marsha Peterman was a brutal experience four years ago. Do I want to repeat it or not?

I wish the answer came as easily as calculus does. But rocket science is simple compared to this.

After school, I head to my job at the Marlborough Free Public Library. Yeah, I realize how perfectly this line of employment goes with my flawlessly dorky image. But it's actually a cool job. Ronnie and Lonnie both work at McDonald's, and they have to perform truly cruddy work like mopping up puke in the bathrooms, wiping down greasy French-fry machines, and sweating over a hot burger grill. All I have to do is handle books. No grease, no puke, and the pay isn't bad.

My parents got me my Range Rover as a birthday present, but I have to pay for my own insurance and gas. Just for the record, New Jersey has the highest car insurance rates, and the lowest gas prices, in the country. We also have the highest property taxes, the highest cost of living, and the lowest unemployment rates.

I've had my library job since I was sixteen. My official title is "page," which sounds truly pathetic, but all that means is that I put books back on the shelves where they belong, check out books for people at the circulation desk, and act as a general gopher for the ravenous reference librarians, which means going out on Dunkin' Donuts latte-and-Munchkin runs three times a day.

When I get there, Janet Pederson, the other page, is behind the circulation desk. She does a double take when she sees me.

"Who're you?" she asks. "And what have you done with Reed Walton? Stuffed him into some goomba's car trunk in Camden?"

"Hey, Janet," I answer with a grin. "Welcome to Reed Walton, the Updated Version."

She smiles. "I go away for the summer to make lanyards with snot-nosed brats in the Poconos, come back, and find out I'm working with a stud."

My mouth twitches. *Stud?*

I know I've gone from dork to human being—zero to five. But zero to ten?

"Well," I say casually, "this must be your lucky day."

Janet smiles even wider. "This is definitely true," she answers.

What is this most unusual situation? Is Janet Pederson flirting with me? I cock my head to one side. I've known Janet since both of us started working at the library last year. She goes to my school, but we don't hang out together or anything. She's cute, actually. I've never been tongue-tied around her before, but I feel a brain freeze coming. Thankfully, Ronnie strolls into the library at that exact moment, saving me from another coconut-trout moment. She rushes over and Janet scowls.

Is Janet *jealous*?

"I wanted to drop this off, Reed," she says breathlessly, handing me a manila envelope.

She touches my arm and again Janet makes a face.

This is getting interesting.

"I gotta get to work," Ronnie says. And, just like that, Ronnie flutters off, leaving me holding the mysterious manila envelope.

Janet smirks at it. "Love letters? Erotic poetry? Marriage proposal?"

Whoa.

"All of the above," I say mischievously. "I've got an official fan club now."

"Really? Do you need a recording secretary? I do great PowerPoint."

This is making me nervous.

I mumble something resembling an excuse/apology, flee the scene, and hurry into the coatroom. Besides, I want to see what Ronnie just gave me. I'll figure out things with Janet later, when I'm thinking straight.

The coatroom's quiet and empty. I lean against the wall and open Ronnie's envelope, trying to forget Janet's astonishing words. I exhale sharply, because what I pull out of Ronnie's envelope is a sheet of paper with this typed at the top:

How to Ask Out a Girl

I start reading.

1. Smile. Even when you're freaking out. Never let 'em see you sweat.

There's scribble next to that in Lonnie's handwriting:

Slather on double-duty deodorant, dawg.

I read on.

2. Watch your posture. Stand up straight. No slouching, cowboy.
3. Make small talk. Say, "How's it goin'?" Hang loose. Chill.

Another scribble from Lonnie:

Make sure deodorant is working.

4. Ask in a casual way, "Wanna go out Saturday?"

Here Lonnie has scribbled something in all caps:

NO NO NO!
REPEAT!
NO NO NO!
Don't EVER EVER EVER give them an out to say no!

Shoot yourself in the groin instead!
Trick them with a multiple-choice question:
Movie or dinner with me Saturday?

Fascinating.

5. After she says yes, say, "Great! I'll call you. What's your
   number?"

From Lonnie:

Eh, no way, Jose. Say: "That's cool, baby. Gimme your number."

6. Get her number.

From Lonnie:

Code Red! Code Red!
Evacuate the area IMMEDIATELY, before she changes her mind!

I stand there feeling numb. I don't know what to make of
this.
I think of Janet.
I take a deep breath.
I run out of the coatroom.

· · ·

Janet's still behind the circulation desk when I emerge from
the coatroom.

"Want to go out next Saturday?"

Once it's out of my mouth, it sounds abrupt and strange. Maybe I should've made small talk. Maybe I should've stuck to the list.

Janet, however, seems fine with it. "Sure, Reed," she says shyly.

Shyly?

It activates the brain freeze, but I fight it long enough to get her number.

Then I remember Lonnie's Number 6 warning:

Code Red! Code Red!
Evacuate the area IMMEDIATELY, before she changes her mind!

I hop away to the periodicals department . . . and promptly crash into a girl carrying a stack of *Glamour* magazines, which explode into a giant mess all over the floor.

"Oh, no! I'm sorry!"

I bend down to help her pick them up. She bends down next to me. Our faces are so close I can see my reflection in her eyes. It leaves me breathless. And, whatever it is she's wearing, her belly is on display, and it's the most beautiful thing I've ever seen.

Something comes over me. I blurt out, "Movie or dinner with me next Friday?"

"Movie," she replies seductively.

. . .

Do girls get it that wearing sexy clothes turns our brains into Farina?

Do they give it any thought at all?

Does it even occur to them?

It reminds me of the time I almost died.

Last summer, Ronnie, Lonnie, and I were down the Shore in Manasquan on one of those perfect beach days.

The lifeguards had hung little triangle-shaped flags everywhere, warning people of dangerous riptides. This expression of caution, of course, only has the effect of switching on the macho gene all guys possess in their DNA.

"Not so far out, guys," Ronnie protested as the three of us splashed into the water.

"It isn't too bad," Lonnie said, but I could tell he was as freaked as I was.

We're all strong swimmers, but I could definitely feel powerful forces in the ocean tugging at me from all directions. Don't take your eye off the waves—not even for a second—I ordered myself.

And that was the exact moment a gorgeous girl in a tiny red bikini popped out of the water like a sensuous mermaid.

"Reed! Reed!" Ronnie shouted. "Watch out! Watch out!"

A wall of water broke over me with such ferocity I could feel my fillings rattle. Next thing I knew, I was being pulverized.

And all because of some mermaid-babe in a tiny red bikini!

Somehow, Ronnie managed to pull me out of the surf.

I couldn't say a single word, much less look at her, for two days afterward.

It was almost a week before I was able to get out the words to thank her.

"I owe you big-time, Ronnie."

"You've been my best friend since kindergarten, Reed. I owe *you* big-time."

That's the kind of friend she is.

. . .

By the time I arrive at my sister's house to babysit after my asking-out experiences in the library, I'm more confused than ever. I've replayed it a hundred times in my head, but I still don't get it.

After the mysterious, sexy girl in the library agreed to a movie, I stuck out my hand and said, "Hi, I'm Reed." I immediately felt ridiculous, offering her my hand like that as if we were accountants meeting at a tax conference in Orlando.

But the girl took my hand, and instead of shaking it, she held it. "I'm Sarah," she purred.

I felt myself being sucked into her seductive eyes. But I snapped out of it, helped her gather the rest of her *Glamour* magazines, got her number, and she left the library.

What had just . . . *happened?*

I'd asked out two girls—in one day—within a span of five minutes.

And they'd both said *yes*.

It was *history*.

I'd used two methods. Lonnie's "trick" question and Ronnie's straight-ahead question. Both had worked.

But what had I learned from these experiences?

Which question was the better question?

Which way was the better way?

It's like I'm at the beginning again. I'm right where I started. I succeeded, but I'm still clueless. I somehow arranged two dates with two girls, but I have no idea how I did it.

I'm not used to this.

In the world I inhabit, things aren't this mystical. Multiple-choice questions on standardized tests have one right answer. Calculus has one right answer. Physics has one right answer. Chemistry has one right answer.

Science is science.

Things add up. Things make sense.

I can't make sense of this at all.

Grandma thinks there's nothing I'm not good at.

But the truth is, if it isn't in a textbook, I'm not good at it.

This is depressing. But my sister doesn't notice my mood when I let myself into her house and make my presence known.

"Uncle Reed's here!" she yells upstairs, then turns to me and begins talking in that mile-a-minute speech pattern used by working moms everywhere. "German chocolate cake in the fridge, leftover veggie pizza, no Coke, make sure they take their multivitamins and brush their teeth and no video games past eight o'clock—gets them too wound up—if you decide to watch *The Lion King* be prepared to discuss the death scene afterward, I recommend *Aladdin* instead, make sure their milk is warmed, you might have to stay in the room with Neil till he falls asleep, Rachel and Danny too, Joely likes to dance to 'Rainbow Connection' before getting into bed. . . ."

My nieces and nephews hurl themselves down the stairs, pile on top of me, and pull me down to the carpet. There are four of them—two girls, two boys—all under the age of eight.

"I lost a tooth!"

"My new dolly poops!"

"I made it to Level Eight today!"

"Can I have three pieces of cake, and three slices of pizza, and three glasses of milk?"

You gotta say one thing about kids. They sure give you a lot of attention.

Christine smiles as she watches them climb all over me.

"They're crazy about you," she says.

"Well, see, I bribe them," I answer. "I have Tootsie Rolls in my pockets."

Christine's husband, Roger, appears beside her, slipping his arm around her waist and looking pleased with himself. It occurs to me that Roger was once my sister's boyfriend, that the two of them dated before getting married. But they've been married since I was seven, so I've never thought of the guy as anything but a husband and provider.

"What's good, yo?" Roger asks.

Talk about wack. Adults using slang to look cool. I could reply, "We straight, dawg, jus' chillin'." But that would make me sound as stupid as him.

"Where are you two lovebirds going?" I ask. I mean this

as a joke, but Christine giggles, and for some reason, this depresses me even more.

"Dinner and dancing," she says.

"And more," Roger teases.

Ick. Gross. Puh-leez.

I do *not* want to think about this. Besides, isn't there something terribly wrong with this picture? Shouldn't my mother-of-four sister be sitting home in crusty sweatpants, inhaling microwavable pizza, and watching Disney movies with her brood? Shouldn't her seventeen-year-old stud of a brother be out on a hot date?

Lonnie's got a hot date—he's probably swapping spit with her in my backseat right now—my grandmother's got a hot date, Ronnie's probably out with Jonathan, even my parents said they were going out tonight.

I'm the only guy in the Garden State stuck at home on a Saturday night with a bunch of overexcited, sticky-fingered rugrats.

I remind myself next weekend will be different. Next weekend my life will change.

Take *that*, Roger.

. . .

We sing songs, eat German chocolate cake, make kettle corn, watch *Aladdin*, play video games, and watch cartoons. They're finally all asleep by ten o'clock.

I'm exhausted. And yet, now that it's quiet and I've got the place to myself, I feel worse than I did before.

I make myself a mug of Dutch hot chocolate and open my

laptop on the coffee table in the living room. There's some old black-and-white movie playing on TCM. *Casablanca*, I think, with Humphrey Bogart.

I write an e-mail to Ronnie and Lonnie. I describe my history-in-the-making events in the library. Then I bombard them with questions.

wut does it mean?
BOTH ur asking-out questions worked!
need answers!
need info!
need nu tip list!
how to go on a date.
hurry!
pronto!
this is an emergency!
send help quickly!

I read over my e-mail before hitting SEND. The panic is a nice touch. I've got plenty of time—a whole week—but I want to get started as soon as possible. I don't want to screw up next weekend.

Loser feelings wash over me when I think about the sad fact that I have to ask my friends how to go on a date with a girl. But, hey, they're experts in the field. Why should I struggle when I can learn from their wisdom and experience?

I spend the rest of the night watching Bogie get the girl, lose the girl, get her again, and lose her again.

How You Doin'?

Exit 4

Sometimes, if the wind is blowing in the right direction, the delicious smells of Grandma's kitchen will carry clear over to Ronnie and Lonnie's house next door. The next morning, Lonnie's on our doorstep on cue, his nostrils having pointed the way.

"Cinnamon," he says definitively.

"The nose knows," I reply, and lead Lonnie into the kitchen.

"Ah, you're right on time, Lonnie," Grandma says. "I was just about to frost my blue-ribbon cinnamon buns."

Lonnie looks like he's waited his whole life to frost Grandma's blue-ribbon cinnamon buns. Grandma helps him get the hang of it and the two of them work together at the counter while I watch with amusement from the kitchen table. If only Marlborough Regional could see this!

Lonnie must be thinking this exact thought, because he keeps throwing me pleading looks. But he's got nothing to worry about. I'll never tell a soul Marlborough Regional's *It Guy* may have a secret love of frosting blue-ribbon cinnamon buns. I wonder why he cares, though. I mean, doesn't Lonnie know anything he does starts a trend? If Marlborough Regional knew their *It Guy* frosted blue-ribbon cinnamon buns, frosting blue-ribbon cinnamon buns would be the next big thing.

When Grandma and Lonnie are done with their frosting work, Grandma gives us each two buns, and we all sit together at the kitchen table. Grandma opens her laptop.

"Now you have to help me with my mottos," she says.

"I got one," Lonnie says, stuffing an entire bun into his mouth. "New Jersey: What's That Smell?"

Grandma laughs.

I add, "Or how about, New Jersey: You Get Used to the Smell."

Grandma shakes her head. "Poor New Jersey. So loathed and so mocked."

"It's so bad, it's good," I say.

Grandma nods. "True. When you're that self-deprecating, you've reached a healthy self-confidence. Just like real life."

We both look at her blankly.

Grandma continues, "Identity, image, finding yourself. That's what it's about, gents."

While I try to understand this, Lonnie puts in, "We can make fun of it 'cause we live here."

I have a feeling Grandma meant something else entirely, but I don't interrupt Lonnie and neither does Grandma.

"New Jersey is actually kinda cool," Lonnie goes on. "We did invent the pork roll."

Grandma grins. "And the drive-in theater."

"And the boardwalk," I say.

"And baseball," Lonnie says.

It's true. New Jersey may be America's armpit—and proud of it—but we did produce those things, not to mention college football, Italian hot dogs, the lightbulb, Bruce Springsteen, Jon Bon Jovi, Queen Latifah, John Travolta, Ray Liotta, Frank Sinatra, and Kelly Ripa. And that's just a partial list.

"How about, New Jersey: Everything You've Heard Is True," Grandma says.

"Or New Jersey: We Can Have You Killed," Lonnie says.

"Or New Jersey: Most of Our Elected Officials Have Not Been Indicted," I say.

Grandma chuckles. "Well, gents, I think you've given me enough to work with. I hereby release you from further motto and frosting duties. And, please, take these with you."

I take the tray of blue-ribbon cinnamon buns, and Lonnie and I go up to my room. When we get there, Lonnie grabs a bun, devours it whole, and says, "Got your e-mail. You telling the truth?"

"Sure," I reply, a bit startled.

"*Two girls*, Reed?"

"Um, yeah, two," I mumble.

Lonnie shakes his head. "Unbelievable."

"What?"

"You ask out two girls and they *both* say yes."

"So? You ask out ten girls a day and they all say yes."

Lonnie gives me a withering look.

"What?" I ask.

He cracks his knuckles noisily. "I get shot down all the time."

I snort. "Not much."

"Yes much."

"But—"

"It happens. Okay? I don't like to broadcast it." He frowns. "Doesn't go with my image."

Image? *Huh.*

The doorbell rings. Half a second later, Ronnie has bounded into the room and flopped onto my bed.

"It isn't calculus," she declares. "That's why you're confused, Reed."

"What?" I mutter.

Ronnie talks very slowly. "There's no right answer, Reed. There isn't one way. Both questions worked because both questions worked. Let it go." She reaches for the last bun, beating Lonnie by only a hair.

"Hog," she mumbles, watching Lonnie chew his bun with cowlike precision.

"I'm a growing boy," he protests.

"You're a growing orca," she retorts.

"Guys," I say. The older we all get, the more they seem to ride each other.

They both turn to me.

"What would we do without you?" Ronnie asks, nibbling

delicately on her bun. "We would've dismembered each other a long time ago."

"Absolutely," Lonnie agrees. "And with plenty of gusto."

"Anyway," I say impatiently.

"Anyway," Lonnie repeats. "She's right. Both asking-out questions worked because they just did. There are no answers here, Reed."

"But, if that's the way it is, how can I replicate it?" I ask.

Ronnie frowns. "Why would you want to 'replicate' it? This isn't a scientific experiment. Maybe one of these girls will end up being your girlfriend. What—you want a harem or something?"

Lonnie snorts. "What's wrong with a harem? And who says he's got to pick from these two? I say he asks out at least twenty more before he makes his final choice."

Ronnie rolls her eyes.

"I don't think I have the stomach for that," I say honestly.

"It gets easier, dude, trust me."

I don't know about that. I can't even bring myself to call these two girls to get directions to their houses. Ronnie leaves after a while, but Lonnie stays to jot down a "telephone script" and rehearse it with me three times before I decide to place the calls. My insides are swirling with overzealous pterodactyls.

Lonnie sits on my bed while I talk to Sarah the belly-bearing sexy girl, shooting me nonstop, unreadable hand signals as if he's landing an F-14 on an aircraft carrier. I finally decide I want him out of my room when I call Janet. He seems put out by this.

"Kicking me out, Reed? Your coach and consultant and best buddy in the world?"

"Nothing personal, Lonnie," I say. "You're making me nervous."

"No more hand signals," he promises.

I run my fingers through my hair distractedly. "I feel like you're scoring me. Like you're going to hold up a card with a number on it."

"Maybe it'll be a perfect ten."

"Or a minus ten."

"You're freaking out, pal."

He's right. I feel like hurling Grandma's blue-ribbon cinnamon buns into the john.

"I don't know if I can go through with this," I say weakly.

He looks concerned. "Chill, dude, chill. It's just two dates with two girls."

"Easy for you to say. You've got an infinite supply. Doesn't matter if you screw up with one or two."

He lets out a laugh. "First of all, you're not gonna screw up. Second, even if you do, *you've* got an infinite supply now too."

"No, I don't."

"Yes, you do," he says firmly. His voice changes, gets more serious. "Third, this isn't a test you can ace or fail, Reed. Nobody's going to give you a grade on it—life's not a school transcript. You can get Cs and Ds instead of A-pluses in real life and still be okay. There's no Ivy League for girls."

I don't know how to answer. Lonnie's a bright guy, but he doesn't take AP classes. He'll go to college, but not Princeton. And yet, he understands me better than I understand myself. What he just said to me is brilliant—pure unadulterated brilliance.

I look down at my sneakers. "I'm not used to not being good at something," I mutter, not knowing how he'll react to this. I don't know how to react to it myself.

"How do you know you're not good at this?" he asks quietly. "Maybe you're the best there ever was."

I smile. "I think *you* get that title."

He laughs. "I don't think so. Besides, Reed, you asked out two girls and they both said yes. You just got off the phone with one of them and you kicked butt."

"But I haven't gone on the dates yet. And remember how I screwed up with Rhonda and Marsha?"

"Forget Rhonda and Marsha. Think Sarah. Think Janet." He gets up. "I'll be at home if you need me."

I reluctantly call Janet after Lonnie leaves. This time, the conversation is much easier. Maybe I'm getting better at this. Or maybe I just know Janet better. Either way, I feel okay about it. I sit on my bed and open my laptop.

ScreamingEagle: rodger.
StudMonkey: told yoo.

ScreamingEagle: now i need 2 actually get thru these d8s.
StudMonkey: get thru? supposed 2 be FUN.
ScreamingEagle: RLY?
StudMonkey: read ur list.

I log off and take out my latest tip list.

How to Go on a Date

1. Do the gentleman thing and open the car door for her.

From Lonnie:

Wait till she's all the way inside before you shut the door or you'll be taking a short trip to the nearest hospital and spending your hot date in the emergency room.

2. Pay for the date unless she insists.

But if you're taking out Donald Trump's daughter, let her pay for everything and order lobster tails and filet mignon.

3. Don't fart, pick your snot locker, scratch, or pop zits.

Do they think I'm a complete moron?

4. Shave extra-extra-closely.

Ready to have your face rubbed by soft girly-hands?

I feel my neck go hot at that one.

5. Trim nose hairs.

Well, *duh*. Who wants to stare at nose hairs?

6. Make sure your feet don't stink. Wear clean socks and clean underwear. Brush and floss. Trim your fingernails. And toenails.

This is beginning to sound like *Introductory Hygiene for Disgusting Boys 101*. Besides, what have my toenails got to do with anything?

7. Wear cologne. Girls like their guy to smell good.

Under no circumstances are you to slap your old man's Old Spice anywhere on your person.

8. Breath mints, breath mints, breath mints. You can't ever have enough breath mints.

I go to Costco that week and buy out nearly the whole section.

I'm taking this seriously.

. . .

I run into a major problem with Number 7.

I've showered, shaved, brushed, flossed, trimmed my nose hairs, trimmed my fingernails, and trimmed my toenails for my date with Sarah on Friday when it dawns on me that I don't own any cologne—and I don't have time to run out and buy any.

Red Alert! Red Alert!

How could I have allowed this to happen?

I've had Ronnie and Lonnie's tip list in front of my face for a week! I have no excuse for screwing this up.

I race into my parents' bathroom with a towel wrapped around my waist and start frantically rummaging through their cabinets, but then I remember I'm not supposed to use anything my dad uses:

*Under no circumstances are you to slap
your old man's Old Spice anywhere on your person.*

Now what?

Heart-stopping panic washes over me.

Should I just . . . skip it?

But what if it's really important?

What if it's *essential*?

I have so little experience with this stuff.

I start to feel way out of my league, biologically incapable, never going to get it . . .

Not Good at This.

No matter how many tip lists Ronnie and Lonnie give me.

I should stick to what I know.

I can't do it.

At that moment, the telephone rings.

"Just checking up on my favorite Jersey guy," Ronnie says pleasantly.

I've never heard anything sweeter.

"Idon'thaveanycologneandIdon'tknowhattodo!" I blurt out in a single sentence, not sure if Ronnie will be able to decipher it.

But she does, of course.

"We're coming right over, Reed."

I throw on a robe, make myself sit on my bed, and don't move a muscle.

The doorbell rings. The cavalry has arrived.

"I'll be the official sniffer," Ronnie announces as she and Lonnie rush into my room. Each of them is carrying a bunch of tiny bottles of different shades of glass. Lonnie lets loose a squirt to the left side of my neck.

"Hey! I wasn't ready!" I protest, jumping out of the way.

He ignores me, and Ronnie leans forward, thrusting her nose between my neck and shoulder.

"*Oooh*, nice," she murmurs.

Her touch gives me uncontrollable chills, and I step away, but Lonnie squirts me again, this time to the right side of my neck.

"Hey!" I cry.

"All part of the pretending package," Lonnie says as Ronnie dives in again.

"*Oooh*, this one's nice too."

"Okay, enough," I say, holding up my hands. "Besides, you're mixing them all up."

"He's right," Ronnie says. She grins at me. "You're gonna smell so good, Reed. Sarah won't be able to keep her hands off you!"

I turn red right down to my perfectly trimmed toes. "What's the pretending package?" I mutter.

"Oh, you're hereby inducted," Lonnie replies. "Into the Hall of Fame."

"Of losers?" I ask.

"Oh, Reed," Ronnie says. "Please."

"Of Guys Pretending to Know What They're Doing," Lonnie answers.

"Pretending?" I ask. "Are you in that too?"

"I'm the president and CEO," Lonnie says with a wink.

"But you know what you're doing," I say.

"No, I'm pretending, like you." He holds up a blue-colored bottle. "This is your Shield of Sham."

I've had enough of stupid riddles for now. "What's he talking about?" I ask Ronnie.

She shrugs. "Beats me. But girls pretend to know what they're doing too."

Lonnie shakes his head. "Girls are *professionals*."

Ronnie snorts. "I bet Sarah's into her eighteenth outfit

by now and she still doesn't know what she's wearing." She checks her watch. "And, speaking of outfits, you better get dressed, Reed."

. . .

My stomach is popping wheelies by the time I arrive at Sarah's house.

I've got three fiery breath mints rattling around in my mouth all at the same time and my tongue feels singed. Between that and Lonnie's cologne, I may croak from olfactory overdose.

I'm early, and I realize Ronnie and Lonnie didn't cover that. I'm not sure if I should drive around the block a few times or just wait on the driveway. I decide to wait. I hope Sarah's family doesn't call the police when they look out their living room windows and spot a guy in a strange car possibly stalking their daughter.

The date hasn't even started yet and I'm already screwing up.

I've got my tip list in my back pocket. It feels like a cheat sheet. I've never cheated on anything in my whole life. I don't really need the list, though, because I've memorized it. After all, memorization is my specialty. I'm probably the only guy in school who can recite all fifty states in alphabetical order.

Besides, most of the things on the list fall under the category of getting ready for the date. There are major, big, problematic holes in the list that I'm just now noticing. For instance, there's nothing about kissing. Kissing! That's the most impor-tant part of a date! Isn't it? Shouldn't I have discussed it with Ronnie and Lonnie? Shouldn't it have merited its own special session? On the other hand, do Ronnie and Lonnie have to show me *everything*? Can't I even figure out how to kiss a girl on my own?

I'm getting nervous. I glance at the house, trying to dis-tract myself. It's nice. There's an old-fashioned trellis along the side that's covered with pink roses. I have a vision of scaling it to reach Sarah's bedroom window. My face flames.

I check my watch. It's time. I open the car door and walk with heavy steps to the front door.

Why has civilized society deemed it necessary to force guys through this ritual torture?

I stand in front of Sarah's door and wipe my clammy hands on my jeans. My palms've started sweating and the glands just won't stop producing. I finally give up, ring the doorbell with my slippery fingers, and realize I haven't breathed in the last five seconds.

I don't know what to do with my hands. This, I am to dis-cover, will be a problem that plagues me all night. Another hole in the list! I shove them into my pockets for now.

What if Sarah's mother comes to the door? What if Sarah's father does? Am I supposed to make intelligent conversation with them? Why wasn't that covered? I feel like I've stepped into an old episode of *Leave It to Beaver*. I see myself sitting on the sofa in Sarah's den, calling her father "sir," drinking choco-late milk, and answering questions about my intentions.

What kind of *Girlfriend Project* is this? Everything that's important is missing! Instead, I'm getting tips on nose hairs and toenails!

But thankfully, after a second or two, Sarah comes to the door. She's wearing tight jeans, high-heeled boots, and a black top trimmed with red lace.

Whoa.

I don't care how many outfits it took to get here—she definitely picked a winner.

"Hi," she says. "You're right on time. I like a guy who doesn't keep me waiting."

I let out the breath I've been holding in one long *whoooosh*. I want to compliment Sarah on her outfit, but I don't want to say something dumb. Yet another item that's missing from Ronnie and Lonnie's list. Should I go for it anyway? Do I trust myself not to screw it up?

"You look great," I mumble.

Hey—that was okay! It was fine! Not suave or anything, but not moronic either.

Sarah smiles widely. "Thanks." She beams and links her arm through mine.

Oh, boy.

I manage to escort her to my car without tripping over my feet or anything, open the door for her, and shut it without maiming her. I walk around to my side and fumble with the lock for so long that Sarah finally reaches over and unlocks it for me.

You win some. You lose some.

I scored with my compliment. But I screwed up with the car door. Maybe this is the way dates are supposed to be. Maybe, at the end of a date, the final tally of scores versus screw-ups determines whether it was a success or failure.

I drive to the twelve-screen multiplex on Route 9. I manage not to wrap my car around any telephone poles or run any red lights. I'm normally a very good driver, but I'm having trouble concentrating on the road.

We talk about school. Sarah says she goes to Marlborough Regional too. I've never seen her there, but it's a huge school. She's a junior.

"Do you play on any teams or anything like that?" I ask her.

"I'm a cheerleader," she says.

I perk up. I'm out with a cheerleader! Way to go, Reed!

"I was in the Homecoming court last year. I was one of the princesses," she adds.

A Homecoming princess? *Woo-hoo!* I'm out with royalty!

She turns to me. "I wouldn't go out with just anybody, you know. I have an image to keep up. I have to consider what people think."

I frown. Something about that sentiment is very, very wrong. Image to keep up? Consider what people think? *What people think?*

I bet I look confused, because she explains, "See, you're a senior, for one, and you're cute, for another, and you've got a car . . ."

Hold on, hold on, hold on. This is *all* wrong. I don't know how to explain it, but Sarah's words are completely, absolutely, positively *all wrong*.

I'm distracted by these comments all evening. We arrive at the movie theater, I pay for two tickets, buy her popcorn and soda, and let her hold my hand during the movie. I would've liked it a lot—it's the first time a girl has held my hand—but I'm too bothered by what she said to me in the car.

After the movie's over, I take her home, don't kiss her goodnight, and don't say I want to see her again.

. . .

"So what? So you're good for her image. So she cares what people think. What—is that a crime? What's the big deal, Reed?"

Lonnie seems frustrated beyond belief. He's holding his head in his hands and shooting me nonstop glances of severe irritation. "Don't you *want* to be the kind of guy girls like to be seen with? What's the problem, pal?"

I look away. Why can't he understand? And why's he so upset about it? It's as if I've personally wounded him.

Ronnie's been quiet the whole time. We're at the Marlborough Diner on Route 34 the next morning for the "Post Game" on my date with Sarah. Did you know New Jersey has the most diners of any state? But the diner was invented in Rhode Island. Rhode Island! I've ordered the Jersey Pig Out—three eggs, three sausage links, three slices of bacon, three buttermilk pancakes, a Mount Everest of home fries—but I've hardly touched it.

"I don't know," I say, staring down at my coffee. "I feel . . . used." I know immediately from Lonnie's expression that this is the wrong thing to say. And think.

"Used?! Used?! *What's wrong with being used?* A gorgeous cheerleader and Homecoming princess wants to use you— and you're having issues with it?" He shakes his head fervently, as if he needs to get my comment out of his ears before it does damage to his brain lobes. "You're killing me, buddy, you're just plain killing me."

"Oh, quit it," Ronnie snaps, making us both stare at her. It's the first thing she's said since we got there. "You're bullying him. Not all guys are in it for the fresh meat, you know."

Lonnie looks shocked. "Fresh meat? Bullying? I'm just trying to help here."

"Well, you're not helping." She gazes at me. "Look, there are all kinds of guys in the world. The ape sitting next to me is obviously one kind." At this, Lonnie makes a face. "But you, Reed, are obviously a different kind—a more sensitive, caring kind." She gives me a smile when she says this, and for some reason, it makes me feel . . . odd.

"Hey!" Lonnie yelps. "I'm as sensitive and caring as the next guy."

Ronnie ignores him. "Forget her, Reed. I know how you feel. You deserve better."

We're quiet for the rest of our meal and barely touch our food.

I can't help feeling I've screwed up.

Again.

I'm not used to this.

. . .

Saturday night. Date Number 2. New driveway. New doorbell.

I feel a little better this time. I guess because I know Janet more. And I feel battle-hardened after my date with Sarah. After some debate, I decide to take her to the same movie. It makes no difference to me. It's a chick flick that girls seem to like, and I don't care about seeing it twice. That's really not the point, is it?

I'm feeling scarred after what happened at breakfast, though. I still don't know why Lonnie reacted the way he did. He's right in a way. I mean, it was just one date. Maybe I misread Sarah's comments. Maybe she didn't mean what I think she meant. Or maybe, like Lonnie said, I'm making too much of a big deal out of it. She's incredibly cute and she obviously likes me. So what if she makes me feel cheap and used? Maybe I'm the one with the problem.

My hands don't get clam up when I stand in front of Janet's door. Maybe I'm getting more experienced. And this time, I don't fumble with the car-door lock either. I'm beginning to relax. This isn't too bad. I'm learning. It's only the second date of my life and everything is a little smoother.

Janet looks different than she normally does at work. She's wearing high-heeled boots like Sarah wore, tight jeans, and a tight sweater. She looks great, and I tell her that. That's getting easier too. She gives me a huge smile.

The conversation in the car flows well and the drive to the

movie theater is fine. We talk about the people we work with at the library, and I make her laugh several times.

When we take our seats inside the theater, a gang of kids races up the aisle from an earlier show, giggling, screaming, fighting, reminding me exactly of my crazed nieces and nephews. An exhausted couple struggles to corral them, without success.

"Snot-nosed brats," Janet mutters. "Disgusting urchins. Repulsive terrors. They ought to be taken out back and shot."

"You don't like kids?" I ask.

Her nostrils flare. "I *detest* kids. They should be allowed to go extinct like the dodo."

I don't kiss her goodnight either.

. . .

Lonnie looks *pained*. "Reed, Reed, Reed," he moans. "You're not marrying her. Why get into kids?"

It's the next day. Breakfast. Marlborough Diner. Post Game.

I don't mean to, but I find myself on the defensive. "It's not about marriage. It's just . . . we didn't click. I can't click with a girl like that. I have four nieces and nephews."

"So what?" he thunders. "Are you planning to bring them with you on dates?" He lays his head down on the table. "I can't take this, buddy." He talks into the tabletop. His words are muffled, but I hear them loud and clear. "You're just being picky now. It's almost like . . ."

"Almost like what?" I ask angrily.

"Almost like you're looking for excuses—lame excuses."

I glare at the top of his head. It's as if I'm putting him through a personal trial or something.

He lifts his head off the table. "Don't you want a girlfriend? Don't you want to kiss a girl?"

I take a sip of my coffee, but I don't taste it. "Sure. But shouldn't I at least like the girl?"

"Not necessarily. You think I've liked every single girl I've kissed or gone out with?"

Ronnie and I both gape at him in surprise.

"What?" he demands. "Is that a felony? Should I be locked up for it?"

"You should definitely be locked up," Ronnie mutters. "You're a menace to society."

Lonnie sighs and stabs his Belgian waffle with his fork. "I guess you're a man of principles, Reed. And you know what? I hope these noble principles are a comfort to you the next time you're babysitting your nieces and nephews alone on a Saturday night."

Ouch. When he puts it that way . . .

"Doesn't love ever come into the picture?" I sputter.

I can't believe I just said this. I may have thought it, but I didn't plan to say it.

"Love?"

Lonnie repeats it with so much revulsion, it's as if I've uttered the dirtiest swear word in the dictionary.

Ronnie throws her brother a look of pure poison. "Oh, Lonnie, why don't you do us all a favor and go hunt a woolly mammoth." She looks at me. "Yes, Reed, love *does* come into the picture. That's what dating is for, and that's why guys like you are such a catch, unlike some people, who'd kiss anything as long as it's still breathing, or maybe they'd just as soon kiss a corpse too."

"Hey!" Lonnie protests. "Don't make me out to be the caveman in this equation. I believe in love as much as the next guy."

We're all quiet for a while. I feel like I should say something to clear the air—or at least change the subject. I venture, "There's another thing too. Janet and I work together. I don't know if I should go out with someone I work with."

Ronnie nods. "That's actually a good point, though you probably should have thought about that before you asked her out."

I hesitate. "And there's more. You know I appreciate everything you guys are doing for me, but . . . those tip lists are missing some important stuff." I start to recite the things I've noticed.

Ronnie looks at me strangely. I can't describe it exactly, except to say it's like a lightbulb has flicked to life in her eyes.

You Talkin' to Me?

Exit 5

1. Would you kiss or date someone you didn't like?
2. Do you expect your dates to make intelligent conversation with your parents when they pick you up?
3. What should your date do if he gets to your house too early?
4. Would you ever date someone you work with?
5. Should boys open car doors for girls?

"I don't know about this, Ronnie," I say after I finish reading the questions. My stomach is performing perfect-ten Olympic somersaults.

"Oh, come on, Reed," she replies. "It's perfect! You get the answers you want, and you possibly get more dates out of it too." She punches me softly in the shoulder. "It's dynamite and you know it."

I frown. "Dynamite for you, maybe," I say. "I'm not sure how dynamite it is for me."

We're in my room later that afternoon, sitting together in front of my laptop on my Amish rug. To my complete astonishment, Ronnie has opened a Web site on my screen called www.thegirlfriendproject.com. A Web site she created, registered, designed, and uploaded—all in the hours between our Post Game breakfast and now.

I move my cursor around the screen restlessly. She's included an introduction before the questions, which reads:

Reed Walton, Ultimate Nice Guy and Ultimate Jersey Guy, needs your help. Answer these questions so he can become an expert on dating. Maybe he'll even pick you to be his girlfriend! Besides, you'll be contributing to a greater body of knowledge. All results will be shared after tabulation.

Can it get any more humiliating than this?

"Ronnie, let's not do this," I say.

"But I worked on it all day," she moans.

"I'll pay you for your trouble."

She grins. "Give it a chance, Reed."

"But it makes me look like a loser."

"No, it doesn't."

"What if nobody participates?" This is the least of my worries, but a guy's got his pride.

"Are you kidding?" she exclaims, snatching one of Grandma's fresh-baked molasses cookies off a plate between us. "It'll be all anyone talks about at school. People love stuff like this. Besides, it's a public service. It's educational. It'll help people. They'll be able to learn from your . . ."

"Screw-ups?"

She smiles. "No."

"That's what you meant." I have to admit—I'm curious about it. But does it have to be on the Internet for the whole planet to see?

She moves closer to me. "Come on, Reed, please?" She kisses my cheek.

I close my eyes. "Okay," I mumble, feeling a tingling sensation in the spot where she kissed me.

She gives me a smile and wriggles away.

"I wish everything was that easy," she says, getting to her feet.

"Putting up a Web site?"

"No, getting a guy to do what I want. That's why you're such a catch, Reed, because you're the nicest guy in the universe."

Yippee-aye-yay for me. What's that ever gotten me?

"Besides, you said you wanted a class with a syllabus and homework assignments. This is sort of like that, isn't it?"

"Maybe, but you said life wasn't a class," I remind her. Everything Lonnie said to me comes back too: *Life's not a transcript. This isn't a test you can ace or fail. You can get Cs and Ds and still be okay. There's no Ivy League for girls.*

"Well, that's true, life's not a class," she replies. "But this sort of makes things more fun."

"Fun for you, maybe, because you're the spectator. I'm the guy making a fool of himself for all the world to see."

She plops down next to me. "Stop thinking of yourself like that! Don't you know how far out you are?" She kisses my cheek again. This time, I pull her into my arms, and she lets me hold her for a good long while. I'm about to do something braver when she wriggles away again.

"Gotta go. Meeting Jonathan at the mall," she says.

Why not me?

. . .

"Reed! Reed!"

It's Dad calling from downstairs. Ronnie left an hour ago and I'm in my room surfing aimlessly. I go to the landing at the top of the stairs. Dad's standing at the bottom looking up at me.

"Can you give your grandmother a ride to the senior center?" he asks me. "It's Bingo Night."

"Sure," I say.

I'm actually glad for something to do. I've done all my homework, there's nothing on TV, Ronnie's out with Jonathan, Lonnie's out shooting baskets with some guys from school.

It's one of those lonely Sunday afternoons when I can't get interested in doing anything on my own—when I feel like everyone except me has something to do—when I would give anything just to have someone I can hang out with on the couch while we watch some old movies.

I pick up the phone twice, first almost calling Janet, then almost calling Sarah. But I hang up both times. Would they say yes to a spur-of-the-moment thing? Maybe. But the truth is, I don't want to be with either of them.

Still, the answer isn't to hole up in my room with my laptop. Besides, my grandmother loves showing me off to all her old-lady friends. I pull on my sneakers and head downstairs to my parents' offices.

My mom and dad are both psychologists. They have a family practice in our house—in an addition built onto the back. They do couples counseling, marital therapy, that sort of thing. Grandma's apartment is in the addition too.

My dad's typing away at his desk when I enter his office. It's a serious-looking room, with a long burgundy couch, a dark coffee table, paintings of barns and cornfields and covered bridges on the walls, and boxes of tissues artfully tucked into corners.

There's floor-to-ceiling shelves on three sides of the room, lined with row after row of books. I scan some of the titles as I wait for my grandmother to come out of her apartment.

Making Your Marriage Work: A Primer for Couples
What Women Want: The Truth from More Than a Hundred Females
What Men Want: The Truth from More Than a Hundred Males
Mars and Venus in the Bedroom: A Guide to Lasting Romance and Passion
Making the Right Choice: How to Choose your Soulmate
Marrying the Right Person: The Proven Scientific Method
Finding the Perfect Partner: From Affection to Zen

Huh. Maybe *I* should read some of these.

"You've read all these books?" I ask my dad.

"Yup. At one time or another," he answers.

"So I guess you're an expert on relationships."

He stops typing and looks at me. Was it something in my voice? Do dads have a gene that tells them their kids want to talk to them about something?

"I know a few things about relationships," he says. "Anything I can help you with?"

"No," I say immediately.

He waits a minute, then starts typing again. Another gene? One that tells him not to push it? Or his training? Should I sit on the coach and let my dad counsel me like he does his patients?

There's a framed photograph of my parents on one of the lower shelves. I look at it closely. They look really happy. They're not much older than me.

"How'd you know Mom was the right person for you?" I ask, then regret it. I don't want to talk about this. Or do I?

He stops typing. "It was a feeling. A gut feeling." He looks at me, waiting, but doesn't say more.

Boy, my dad is *good*. He knows exactly when to stop and when to go. He knows that if he says too much, or seems too interested, I'll clam up. But he also knows if he doesn't tell me enough, I'll want more.

But I'm on to him. I don't say anything else. And Grandma comes through the door at the end of the hallway, smelling like lilacs and saving the day. Or not? She loops her arm through mine.

"Lucky me—I've got a hot date tonight," she says, beaming at me.

"Reed's just dropping you off," my dad says with a laugh. "I'll pick you up when you're done."

"Oh, too bad," she says.

"Now, Grandma, you don't want to make your friends too jealous," I tease.

"Oh, but I do, Reed, I do," she replies.

This is our running gag.

I help Grandma out of the house and into my car. She sighs happily.

"You should be given a trophy for Best Grandson in the World."

"How about prize money? Then I can buy a Mustang and get all the girls I want."

She laughs. "You don't need a Mustang to get girls, Reed. You're a catch."

A catch. Everyone keeps telling me that. If I hear it one more time, I'll barf. Funny thing is, neither my grandmother nor my parents have made much of the new and improved me. Grandma's been calling me a "handsome boy" since I was fourteen, but I guess that's what grandmothers do.

I pull out of the driveway. I feel like talking.

"Have you ever been bad at something, Grandma?" I ask. "Have you ever tried to do something that you kept screwing up?"

"Oh, heavens, yes," she says, turning to me. "Baking."

"Baking?"

"I was awful at it in the beginning. I burned my first cake to a crisp. A crisp, I tell you."

"But you're so good. That's what you do."

"That's because I kept trying. I didn't give up."

I don't say anything. Grandma continues to look at me, but she doesn't ask me what I'm getting at. Maybe that's why I've always felt so comfortable around her. She never pushes me. I imagine this is what it's like to sit at a bar and spill your guts to a friendly bartender.

"Didn't you wonder if you'd ever get it right?" I finally ask.

She nods. "Oh, yes. But I believed in myself."

We arrive at the senior center. I help her inside the building, stand around with her in the lobby before Bingo starts, and let her brag about me.

"Maybe you'll stay for a few rounds," one of the old ladies says to me.

"I'd love to, but I have too much to do," I say, which is a bald-faced lie on both counts. I have absolutely nothing to do, but I can't play Bingo at the senior center on a Sunday afternoon. It might be all right, but come on. How low do I have to go?

I say good-bye to Grandma and, on a whim, drive to the Woodrow Wilson Basketball Courts at the George Washington Municipal Park to see if I can find Lonnie. But he isn't there.

That girl's there, however, shooting baskets by herself. I sit in the car and watch her.

Who is she?

What kind of guys does she like?

Does she think kids should be allowed to go extinct like the dodo? Does she have an image to keep up?

In the last few days, I successfully asked out two girls. Why can't I go up to her?

I'm still getting used to the idea that I look different than I used to look. I know I'm not repulsive. But cute? A stud? Good for somebody's image? How is it possible? I feel the same way I always did—like a dorky loser who girls laugh at.

"I wish I could go up to you and talk to you," I say out loud in the car. "But I can't. I'm too scared. Well, I did ask out two girls and they both said yes. Things didn't work out, though." I pause. "When I was a freshman, this girl I really liked a lot—Marsha Peterman—turned my life into a living nightmare. See, she didn't just shoot me down, she did that giggle-and-point-at-the-loser-with-her-girlfriends thing whenever I walked by for weeks afterward."

I think back to Marsha's incredible cruelty. "Are you the kind of girl who does stuff like that?" I shake my head. "Did Marsha think I didn't notice that? Did she think it wouldn't bother me? *Why do girls do that?*"

And why did I still like her?

. . .

New Jersey definitely has an image problem.

This has always interested me, but it's downright fascinating now. Maybe I'm mental, but I'm seeing . . . *parallels.*

Or maybe it's because I was born here, I'm going to college here, and I'll probably die here. Ronnie says I'm the Ultimate

Jersey Guy. I wrote an essay about this last year that was published in our local newspaper, *The Asbury Park Press*.

New Jersey and Us
Perfect or Not?

You know you're from Jersey when . . .
- You don't think "What exit?" jokes are funny.
- There's always one kid in every class named Tony.
- You've never pumped your own gas.
- You know how to navigate a circle and a jug handle.
- You know the two things above have to do with driving.

But New Jersey is actually cool.

Then I listed all the good things about the Garden State. See, actually, New Jersey has a lot going for it. For instance, we're home to the Statue of Liberty—*not* that other state you're thinking of. Jersey tomatoes and Jersey corn are the best you can buy. We have the most Revolutionary War sites of any state. And the game Monopoly is named for the streets of Atlantic City.

But we keep pretty quiet about all those things. We're a pretty cool state, but we don't want anyone to know about it.

It definitely makes me think of other things . . .

I'm thinking about it in study hall a few days later. Study hall is the only class Ronnie and I have together. It's in the library. Ronnie's at one of the library terminals typing away; I'm sitting next to her, doing my AP Calculus homework.

She lets out a cry of excitement. "Omygosh! We got our first posts at thegirlfriendproject.com!" She turns to me. "I told you it would work! Told you, told you, told you!"

I'm shocked, but I pretend to be bored instead. "I need a nap," I say, and yawn loudly.

Ronnie punches me softly in the arm. "Nice try." Then she happens to catch a glimpse of my AP Calculus homework. She reads aloud:

"The graph of $x + 4xy - y = 3$ is continuous for all real numbers except for one value, $x = c$. Use the rate of change of the equation to help you find c and classify the discontinuity you find in the derivative."

She shakes her head as she studies the equations I've scribbled in my notebook. "How do you do it, Reed? How does this stuff make any sense to you?"

"It isn't so bad," I say.

She places her hands on either side of my head. "You've got a gorgeous brain in there, Reed."

I want to take her hands in mine. I want to bring them to my lips and kiss them.

But the bell rings.

Who am I kidding? I wouldn't have done that anyway—bell or no bell.

I'm a wuss.

We get up and head out of the library together.

"I'm so excited for you, Reed! I can't wait to read the posts!" She turns to me and gives me a big hug.

I bury my face in her hair. It smells delicious. Like strawberries.

"Hey, hands off my girl, man."

It's Jonathan, Ronnie's big, hairy, varsity-wrestler, pea-brain boyfriend, his meaty paws grabbing for her. I let Ronnie go, hiding my scowl.

"Oh, put a sock in it, Jonathan," Ronnie growls. "It's only Reed."

Only Reed.

Only Reed.

I walk away, beyond hurt, beyond fuming.

She comes after me.

"Reed, I didn't mean it like that." She throws her arms around me again.

I forgive her on the spot. I can't help it. I hug her tightly and ignore the outrage on Jonathan's face.

. . .

We're in my room after school reading the posts at www.thegirlfriendproject.com. There are more than I expected, and they're kind of fun, in a weird way.

1. Would you kiss or date someone you didn't like?

DirtyGirl: if he was johnny depp

greenfrog: yea!

sk8erboy: maybe kiss but not d8

HotStud: i kiss or d8 anything that moves

allstar: yea because i might like him once I kissed him

floweringgarlic: i'd kiss reed in a minute

BabeHunter: ofc! do u even have 2 ask?

2. Do you expect your dates to make intelligent conversation
   with your parents when they pick you up?

monster11: depends on ur definition of intelligent

floweringgarlic: i always get the door be4 they du

DirtyGirl: my dad lives 4 that

FallenAngel: i expect them 2 make *un*intelligent
conversation

wicked: my d8es not intelligent!

3. What should your date do if he gets to your house too
   early?

floweringgarlic: cmon in water's fine.

cranialtornado45: nothing perverted

allstar: test his breath 1 more time

wrsssatty: meditate. think positive thoughts. be at 1 w/the
universe.

el sexy: get me a grande caramel mocha decaf latte no
foam w/ soy milk

4. Would you ever date someone you work with?

DirtyGirl: if he looked like johnny depp
Mightyviking: no.2 much trouble
LonerWolf: if u br8k up 1 of u has to quit
wrsssatty: if i was the boss
wicked: pretty stupid idea
monster11: not if i needed the paycheck
HotStud: if she's sexilicious
BabeHunter: she might be the luv of my life so ya

5. Should boys open car doors for girls?

HotStud: what happened to feminism? how bout the girl opens car door for me?
floweringgarlic: it's nice
monster11: there r more important things 2 do
FallenAngel: fine by me
allstar: ofc! regular doors too
DirtyGirl: nbd
el sexy: this won't matter once we start driving space ships. the doors will open by voice lk star trek

And, in the comments section, there are these gems:

floweringgarlic: i'm a nice jersey girl looking 4 nice jersey guy
DirtyGirl: pick me reed!!!!!!

allstar: i'd go out w/ reed!!!!! he's a QT!!!!!
HotStud: hey reed gr8 idea! can i steal it?
BabeHunter: are u a genius or something?

"It looks like we're getting guys and girls," Ronnie says. "Which is great." She shakes her head. "All I did was post one message on the school Listserv."

"And it looks like you might get a few dates out of it," Lonnie adds. "Which is all well and good, but what if they're dogs?"

Ronnie sighs. "Oh, Lonnie, why do you have to be such a pot-bellied porker?"

"Hey, I think that's a legitimate concern. Right, buddy?"

I don't reply, because I don't feel like I have the right to comment on this, what with my special history.

"Fine," Ronnie relents, "we'll ask them to post photos."

"No, no," I say. "It's okay."

"Woof! Woof!" Lonnie yelps.

"Come on, Lonnie, you don't mean that," I say.

He gives me a sheepish look. "Yeah, okay. But, hey, if this gets too big for you, you mind sharing some of the action?"

This is something new—Lonnie coming to me for dates. "Um, sure."

"So, what do you think, Reed?" Ronnie asks.

I can't help smiling. "It's pretty interesting," I say.

Most of the posts are tongue-in-cheek, but some are kind of insightful. They're not earth shattering, but they're not completely worthless either. And frankly, I'm shocked that floweringgarlic, DirtyGirl, and allstar—whoever they are—want to go out with me.

"You're going to be the most popular guy in school!" Ronnie gushes. She scrolls through the posts again. "I wonder who's who. . . ."

. . .

Things get pretty weird that week.

People I don't know say hello to me in school. A pack of sophomore girls in identical tight jeans giggle as I walk by. And someone has scrawled "Pick Me!" on my locker in bright red lipstick. Trying to smear it off with the back of my hand only makes it worse. I finally have to ask the janitor for help, and it takes three foul-smelling detergents to make it go away.

I'm flabbergasted. By third period of the fourth day, my nerves are shot. Now I know why celebrities punch out paparazzi.

Rhonda Wharton lingers at my locker between first and second periods on the fifth day as I'm getting ready to make a run for AP Biology.

"I checked out your Web site, Reed," she says shyly, batting her eyelashes at me. Batting her eyelashes at me! She starts to say something four times as I absently pull textbooks out of my locker. But she stops each time. I wait for her to finish, but if I don't leave in the next two seconds, I'll be late. As it is, I've got to sprint clear over to the other side of the building.

"I'm sorry, Rhonda, I gotta go," I finally mutter. "Catch ya later?"

She looks so disappointed I want to rub my eyes in disbelief. Rhonda Wharton, a girl I've secretly admired from afar since we were twelve years old, doesn't want me to leave? I turn to go, but she puts a hand on my arm, which has the effect of instantly stopping me in my tracks.

"You . . . Me . . . We . . . ," she murmurs.

I like the sound of this a lot, but it also makes me nervous. Still, I don't move a muscle. There's no way I'm shrugging off Rhonda Wharton—not even if I get a detention for being late. But Rhonda lets me go and doesn't say anything more, so I rush off, making it to class by a hair.

I don't get it.

Rhonda Wharton's never given me the time of day. Now she's practically stalking me.

What's happening?

Celebrity? Fame? Hype? Image?

Whatever it is, there's something not right about it.

I know I sound like a broken record, but I have to say it again.

I'm the same guy.

I'm shaking my head when I meet Ronnie and Lonnie for lunch at our usual table in the school cafeteria. I take one bite of my soggy round pizza-for-one and decide my stomach can't handle any more. Besides, the cheese tastes fake, the sauce is soupy, and the pizza's still frozen in the middle. There's a Law of the Universe out there, I know, that demands school cafeterias serve inedible food. Luckier districts may have Taco Bell,

Pizza Hut, a[...]Donald's in the[...]
menu is still trapped in a lunchtime [...]

I tell Ronnie and Lonnie everything about my day. Ronnie's eyes grow rounder and rounder.

"I knew it!" she cries excitedly. "I knew it, I knew it, I
knew it."

"But this is no different than Floyd Flavin getting arrested
last year," I say. "It's hype—all hype." I think this is a mature
attitude, but Lonnie's not impressed.

"Go with it, dude," he says, ripping a chunk out of my pizza,
shoving it into his mouth, and grimacing. "Milk it."

"But it's not real, Lonnie, it's hype."

"So what?" There's an annoyance in his voice—an annoyance I'm coming to know well since we started this *Girlfriend
Project*. "The public's fickle. Act on the moment. You're the fla-
vor of the month. Next month someone else will be *It*."

I try not to frown, but I can't help thinking that the differ-
ences between the two of us have been highlighted so much in
the past few weeks it's astounding we're friends at all. When
did Lonnie become so . . . superficial? Was he always like this?
On the other hand, who am I to judge? The last thing I want to
be is a whiny, ungrateful, goody-two-shoes Boy Scout—even
though technically I am a Boy Scout.

Rhonda Wharton walks across the school cafeteria
toward our table. She's hugging her textbooks to her chest
nervously, but this shy-schoolgirl thing only makes her more
adorable.

I stare down at my tray as she approaches our table,

...d the rest of ... od in the li-
... options for so long I fail to notice
Rhonda standing quietly in front of our table, shifting uncomfortably from foot to foot, waiting for me to look up. When I don't, she whispers my name, and that's when it dawns on me. She's walked clear across the school cafeteria, in plain view of everybody, to see *me*.

I gaze up at her with my mouth open. Then I come to my senses. It isn't right for her to stand there, looking so awkward and uneasy, while I'm sitting down. So I scramble to my feet, so quickly I almost knock over my chair. It isn't a smooth gesture, but I think she appreciates it anyway, because she smiles.

I shoot my friends a quick glance. It lasts for only a second, but I manage to catch Lonnie's mischievous wink and a go-for-it-Reed signal from Ronnie.

I decide in that instant I've been too hard on them, especially on Lonnie. He's my best friend—he only wants to help me. I decide I'm going to do what he wants. I'm going to make him proud. I inhale deeply, take Rhonda's elbow, and lead her to a quiet corner where we can talk privately. It takes everything out of me to do this, but I'm glad I do. In a way, it's downright suave. And Rhonda seems to appreciate it too, because she's practically beaming at me.

She fastens me with doe eyes that make me want to melt on the spot. "Reed, will you . . . Can you . . . Do you think you can . . . give me a ride home today . . . after school?"

I smile. "It would be my pleasure, Rhonda. Reed's Car Service is always at *your* service."

Rhonda giggles, but I have to wonder, Where on earth did *that* come from? That wasn't me talking at all. That was . . . Lonnie.

It sure sounded good, though.

. . .

Rhonda lives a ways from school in one of those new housing developments on the edge of Marlborough. McMansions, I call them. The land on which Rhonda's house is built used to be an apple orchard, but the only trace of that quaint past these days is the name of the development: Apple Tree Estates.

I guess I don't have to tell you New Jersey is the most densely populated state in the country. And we have the most shopping malls per square mile of any area in the world.

On the other hand, did you know we have more racehorses than Kentucky does?

We're pretty complicated, I guess.

Like a lot of other things.

Rhonda and I make awkward small talk on the way to her house. Honestly, I'm relieved when I finally pull into her driveway. I can't take much more of this. It's nerve-wracking. Besides, I don't have any breath mints on me.

"Do you want to . . . come in?" Rhonda asks, and her cheeks immediately turn scarlet.

I freeze. My mouth replies, "I have to go to work."

This is a completely true statement, but the way it comes out sounds like I'm making excuses, like I don't want to come in at all, which is partly true and partly false. Of course I want to come in! On the other hand, I'll probably drop dead before I reach the front door. I've never, ever been inside a girl's house—not counting Ronnie—and I don't know the first thing about it. This is too much. I need a tip list! And some breath mints!

"Oh, okay," Rhonda mumbles, staring down at her lap, looking hurt.

For crying out loud!

Why am I so inept?

Can't I say something? Can't I do something?

"I'm s-sorry," I stammer, then, "Maybe another time?"

This works. Rhonda smiles.

Then she slides forward and tries to kiss me.

I let out a cry of surprise and turn my head in the wrong direction. Rhonda ends up with a mouthful of my hair. She pulls back, her face purple with embarrassment.

I want to die. Somebody, please, put me out of my misery.

Rhonda mumbles something I can't understand, opens her door, and practically runs into the house.

I sit on her driveway and bang my head on the steering wheel.

· · ·

But my rotten day's still not over. Because when I get to work, Janet's got some choice words for me.

"You should've just said so," she snarls when I say hello to her. "About not going out with someone you work with. How was I supposed to know that? I had no idea. If you'd just told me . . . it's so inconsiderate. You could've said something, you know."

I stand there and take her abuse without uttering a single word in my defense, but what's going through my mind is this:

The priesthood is looking better than ever.

When I get home, Grandma is at the kitchen table typing away on her laptop, and I'm glad, because I need to talk to someone.

"I made your favorite, Reed," she says with a smile, indicating a peanut butter pie on the counter.

"Wow," I reply. This is *exactly* what I need. I cut myself a slice and carry it to the kitchen table.

"New Jersey," Grandma says as I sit down beside her, "The Traffic Will Kill You. Have a Nice Day."

"New Jersey," I say, "Where the Finger Is the Official State Greeting."

Grandma laughs. "Another winner." She types away.

I wait for her to finish, then say, "Grandma, remember that time you said . . . New Jersey had an . . . identity problem?"

She looks up, giving me her full attention.

I'm not sure where I'm going with this, but I continue, "Well, um, why is that?"

I wonder if she knows what I'm getting at. She looks at me thoughtfully for a minute, then answers, "I guess it's that New Jersey doesn't know where it wants to go. It's poised on a period of great change. And change is difficult."

That's it exactly!

Grandma eyes me closely. "We can't grow without change, Reed. Yet growing is painful. Maybe that's why we call it 'growing pains.'"

"Growing pains," I repeat slowly.

"We *have* to grow, Reed," Grandma goes on. "Without growth, we stagnate."

This is getting murky, but it's helpful, and I have a feeling Grandma knows it.

"New Jersey," I say, feeling suddenly inspired, "We'll Let You Know When We Figure It Out."

"New Jersey," Grandma responds, "Our Grandsons Are Geniuses."

I feel a little better about everything. But, unfortunately, it doesn't last.

The following week is exactly the same as the week before. People I don't know say hello to me in school, sophomore girls giggle, freshman boys applaud, hoot, and high-five me.

We get more posts, more requests for dates with me, and pleas for more survey questions. I cannot for the life of me figure out how one simple Web page—five measly questions—has caused such a stir.

"It's not that, Reed," Ronnie explains to me when we're on my Amish rug a week and a half later, reading everything. "It's not the questions. It's you—you advertising that you're looking for a girlfriend—your *Girlfriend Project*."

"Every guy in America's looking for a girlfriend," I say. "Why am I getting all the attention?"

"That's not true," Ronnie replies. "Lots of guys are just looking for *action*. You want a *commitment*. Combine that with you being cute and sweet and smart . . ."

I lower my eyes, even though this is music to my ears, especially from her.

"I'm not surprised at all," Ronnie goes on. "It's taken on a life of its own."

And this brings us to the Big Issue. "Well," I mumble, "then I think it's time to kill it, Ronnie."

"Kill it?" She looks absolutely scandalized. "No way."

"But this Web site is making my life miserable!" I say, not meaning to sound so pathetic, but it's the truth.

Ronnie snorts. "Oh, sure, Reed, it's so miserable having girls throw themselves at you."

I must be a dork down to my bone marrow, because I know other guys would kill for this setup. But this isn't what I wanted at all. How can I make her understand that?

"I wanted a girlfriend, Ronnie, remember? Not girls throwing themselves at me."

"But you've got to date girls to find a girlfriend."

What I want to say is, "I already know who I want."

Instead I say, "I don't want to date girls."

She gazes at me for a long time. I hope she'll finally get it. But instead, she asks, "Are you gay?"

"No!"

"It's okay if you are . . ."

"I'm not!"

She looks puzzled. "I don't understand, Reed, really. Why don't you want to date girls?"

Just tell her.

"Because . . . because . . ."

She moves closer to me. "Because you're shy and nervous and confused?"

Yes, yes, and yes. But that's not it at all.

"You can't give up, Reed, you have to keep trying. I know it's hard for you. You're learning."

"But everything's coming out wrong!" I yell.

It had nearly killed me to tell Lonnie about the botched-up kiss with Rhonda the other day. It nearly killed him too. I think he's downright revolted by me now.

"Take it off, Ronnie," I say, then feel my face flame. That sounds like something other than what I intended. I wonder if that's how Ronnie will hear it. But she doesn't, and even though it's absurd, that really depresses me.

"No, Reed, I'm not taking it off. The Web site stays."

"But it's my life you're playing with!"

"You just need a little help, that's all."

"A little help? I can't even kiss a girl!"

I'm losing it. I don't want to lose it. Maybe in front of Lonnie, but not in front of her.

"You may think you're beyond help, but everyone else thinks differently. Samantha Spinner invited you to her party this weekend, remember? That's something."

"I don't care."

"You're hot now."

"Aren't you listening? I said, I don't care." I hate the tone I'm using with her, but I'm basically at my wit's end. I peer at her to see how out-of-line I am. She doesn't look angry. She looks concerned.

She touches my hair. I wish she'd stop touching me. It only makes things worse.

"Please give it more time. A few weeks? Please, Reed?"

"Okay," I mutter in defeat.

Has Ronnie ever noticed she can make me do anything she wants?

. . .

I've always liked Ronnie. A lot. A whole lot.

But that doesn't mean I ever expected anything.

She kept getting prettier and prettier, more and more popular, more and more desirable, more and more out of my league.

She's always hugged me, touched me, kissed my cheek, played with my hair. I knew she meant nothing by it. I was probably like another brother to her.

I had resigned myself to the fact that I'd never get her in a million years. I had accepted it.

Until now.

The fact of the matter is, she's the girlfriend I want at the end of this dumb *Girlfriend Project.*

It's no contest.

I would never have allowed myself to think this before all of this started. But now I can't help it.

I can't stop thinking that maybe I have a chance with her now.

Maybe.

On the other hand, she has a serious boyfriend. She's always had serious boyfriends.

I suppose I could get into other girls. I would've liked kissing Rhonda Wharton. I liked Marsha Peterman for years. I thought Janet and Sarah were both cute.

But Ronnie's the one I really want.

Ronnie's the one who's always been my friend; the one who sent me Valentines, the one who saw beyond my glasses and braces and dorkiness, the one who saved me from drowning.

Literally. And in general.

Ronnie gets me.

I wish I could get her.

But this stupid Web site isn't getting me closer to that.

In fact, it's doing the opposite.

. . .

I go through an hour's version of *I Have Nothing to Wear!* with Lonnie before Samantha Spinner's party. I don't mean me. I'm fine in my favorite jeans and a cargo shirt. I mean *him.*

"Too Afghanistan," he says of a pair of desert-camouflage pants.

"Too Korea," he says of a pair of olive cargo pants.

"Too South Bronx," he says of a pair of torn jeans.

"Lonnie, you're worse than a girl," I say.

"I didn't ask you if I was fat," he counters. "Besides, you're the only one who gets to see the real Lonnie White in all his insecure glory."

That's true. The real world only gets to see His Coolness. It's only me who gets to see the real guy under that. Of all people, I should know better than to give him a hard time about it.

"Anyway," Lonnie goes on, "I hear Deena will be there."

"You want Deena back?"

"Yup."

"Why don't you call her?"

"Because she might say no, genius."

"To *you?*"

"I ain't an American Idol, Reed."

"Why do you need to be so cool, Lonnie?" I ask.

Lonnie pauses, and I expect another smart reply, but instead, he says, "Because people expect it."

"Your public?" I say, half-joking but also half-serious.

"You think it's easy being me?" he asks, and his voice is serious.

It makes me think about all the attention I've been getting lately. It's nice, I suppose, but it's also hard. Lonnie must pick up on this thought, because he says, "I bet you sometimes wish for your dork days back, Reed."

I shift uncomfortably. "It's less confusing."

Lonnie looks disgusted. "Enough of this Oprah crap, let's go to the party already."

I guess Lonnie's sensitive side has limits. But it's easier talking to Ronnie about this kind of stuff anyway.

Samantha Spinner's party is one of those events that separates the nerds from the beautiful people. If you're here, you're here, if you know what I mean.

Lonnie and I arrive just after 10 p.m. There are so many cars parked along the road I have to find a spot for my Range Rover three blocks away.

Samantha's house is huge and fancy, with an iron gate in front of it and a giant brick mailbox. There are people everywhere, all over the lawns, on the curved driveway, crowded by the front doors. Lonnie says hello to a gazillion girls, and shockingly, they all seem to know me too.

Now, you may wonder why I wasn't the happy recipient of Lonnie's leftovers all these years. But really, with him as the main course, who'd look at me? I wasn't good enough to be his doggie bag.

When we get inside Samantha's house, we're blasted with loud music. In the kitchen, people are playing a drinking game. Other people are leaning against the counters, talking. I don't know if Samantha's parents are around or not, but even though she's not serving, people always bring their own.

In the living room, a bunch of girls in tight jeans are dancing—bumping and grinding to the music. Lonnie and I stand in the doorway and watch them. I think every guy in the place is watching them.

"Enjoying the entertainment?" someone asks Lonnie.

I look down to see Deena Winters, Lonnie's ex-girlfriend, standing next to him.

Lonnie puts his arm around her. "Actually, I prefer my entertainment to be the one-on-one kind," he says.

A few hours ago, he was a nervous wreck about this girl. Now he's so smooth, so confident, so sure of himself; it makes me wonder which Lonnie is the real one.

Where does it all come from? Why don't I ever feel that way?

"Catch ya later, buddy," he says to me with a wink.

Oh, great. Now he could be occupied for hours. I'm Lonnie's ride home—which means I'm stuck here—by myself. Where's Ronnie? She's supposed to be here with Jonathan. I stand there wondering what to do with myself when a bouncy girl with fiery red hair waltzes over.

"You're that guy, aren't you?" she asks.

I look behind me. She laughs, thinking I did that on purpose.

"You should put your picture on your site. You'd get even more posts. But I guess you don't need any more. So, have you decided? Have you found the right girl?"

"No," I say, understanding now. "Not yet." I still can't get used to comments like this about my appearance.

The girl smiles. She's got a great body. I'm about to ask for her name when someone walks right-smack into me. I look down into the lovely face of Marsha Peterman. She's glassy-eyed, and I realize she's probably drunk. She wobbles forward, I lean toward her instinctively, and she falls right into my arms.

The bouncy redhead makes a face. "Nice act," she mutters, and walks away.

But Marsha's not acting. She's sloshed. She's hanging onto my neck, pressing herself against me, staring steadily into my eyes.

Normally, this would be a very thrilling moment for me. But I'm afraid she's going to puke.

"Are you okay?" I ask. "Do you need a bathroom?"

"Can we sit down?" she slurs.

I help her to a nearby sofa. Someone's just gotten up and left a deep indentation behind. I sink into the cushions and Marsha plops into my lap and wraps herself around me.

Whoa.

This is the closest I've ever been to a girl. Even Ronnie has never sat in my lap. It's *great*. But what do I do now? Is Marsha going to fall asleep on top of me? On the other hand, who cares? There's no one here I especially want to see. This is perfect, really. I can sit here and wait for Lonnie. And in the meantime, I'll have a hot girl sleeping on me. I remind myself that a month ago, I would've gladly committed murder to have Marsha Peterman sprawled drunkenly across my lap like this.

So I sit there, holding Marsha and hoping she doesn't vomit. Other girls walk by. Some smile, others scowl at Marsha's lifeless body. I nod to a few people I know from school. Several people comment I must've found my girl.

Marsha suddenly comes to life and I brace myself for an indignant reaction. I imagine her slapping me across the face, accusing me of pawing her while she was helpless, reminding me I brought up a painful trout memory for her.

Instead, she leans forward and puckers her lips.

She wants to kiss me.

For seventeen years, no girl has ever gotten close to my face. Now two girls in the same month have wanted to kiss me.

But do I really want my very first kiss to be with a drunk girl with beer breath?

On the other hand, this is my chance to redeem myself. To do what I couldn't do with Rhonda Wharton.

I know who I want my first kiss to be. But that's as likely to happen tonight as traveling to Mars.

I have to kiss a girl sometime. Why not Marsha? Why shouldn't she be my first?

I don't really know what I'm doing, but I guess some kind of instinct takes over. I close my eyes, lean forward, and kiss Marsha. She tightens her arms around my neck and the next thing I know, we're energetically sucking face. I get so into it I forget we're at a party with people around. The kiss goes on and on, and Marsha makes adorable moaning noises that I hope mean she likes what I'm doing. I don't want to stop, and I guess Marsha doesn't either, because we don't pull apart until it's clear we both need oxygen.

Kissing is *awesome*!

It's too bad it took me this long to find that out. I feel like there should be trumpets and fireworks and marching bands. I can't believe I've *finally* kissed a girl.

Marsha gazes at me with wonder in her eyes. Could it be I did something right for a change? What's she thinking? Will she even remember this tomorrow?

"Oh, Reed," she sighs. "That was . . ."

Nice? Not nice?

Good? Bad?

Great? Terrible?

But she doesn't finish. Instead, she leans in for more.

Well, at least she knows who I am. We kiss a second time, and this time, it lasts even longer.

When we finally come up for air, I notice I have an audience.

Lonnie's standing in the doorway with Deena on his arm. He gives me a thumbs-up sign.

Rhonda Wharton's across the room with her eyes narrowed at me.

The bouncy redhead, surrounded by other bouncy-looking girls, nods at me knowingly.

And Ronnie, with Jonathan behind her, is watching me from the other side of the room with an expression that makes me gulp.

Confusion?

Envy?

No. It's got to be my imagination.

It's *got* to be.

Still, I wish I could take it all back. And start over.

1. Would you kiss someone with beer breath?
2. What would you do if a guy asked you out like this: 'Movie or dinner with me Saturday night'?
3. Should guys pay?
4. If a guy doesn't kiss you on your first date, what does that mean?
5. Should girls ask out guys?

"So, it was pretty outta sight, huh?"

I wish Ronnie would drop it, but all she's wanted to talk about is my first kiss with Marsha Peterman, which ended up being more like eighteen first kisses. Marsha kept wanting more and more of it—the girl was insatiable!—so I kept giving it to her. It was *awesome*. I even forgot about the audience—including Ronnie. And in the end, Lonnie had to wait for *me*.

But I don't want to talk about it with Ronnie now. We're in her room the day after Samantha Spinner's party. Connie, Ronnie's white girl cat, is in her lap. Johnnie, the black guy cat, is in mine. We're cross-legged on the carpet, leaning against the wall, with both felines purring away.

"The beer breath was kind of tough," I say.

"Breath mints, Reed."

"What was I supposed to do—shove one in her mouth?"

"Why not? Anyway, the next time you kiss her, I'm sure she'll be minty fresh."

"The next time?"

"Yeah. Aren't you gonna ask her out?"

"I'm not sure," I say.

She sighs. "Oh, you're not one of those people, are you, Reed?"

"What people?"

"The kind of people your parents see in therapy. The kind of people who like somebody—until that person likes them back."

"No, it's not that."

"Then what is it?"

I take a deep breath. "I think I like someone else."

"Who?"

When I don't reply, she asks, "What—is it a secret?" Connie jumps out of her lap, and Ronnie crawls toward me. "Tell me, or face the consequences, Reed."

I grin at her.

"Okay, you asked for it." She starts tickling me.

I tickle her back and soon we're laughing and rolling around the carpet together.

We've wrestled since we were kids, so this isn't especially out-of-the-ordinary behavior. I wish I could show her things are different now, though. I start to kiss her neck amorously, but it's no good. This is brave of me, and under different circumstances, it might have clearly signaled my feelings. But because it comes on the heels of our wrestling, it feels playful rather than romantic. Ronnie giggles and bats me away.

If I could just kiss her for real, kiss her like I did Marsha Peterman, there'd be no doubt in her mind. But she pushes me off, gets to her feet, and says, "Jonathan'll be here any minute."

Why does this keep happening to me?

. . .

I pick up Lonnie later that afternoon at his job at McDonald's and we go to the Freehold Raceway Mall. Ronnie has the day off and she's out with her pet gorilla, uh, Jonathan.

Even in grease and crud, Lonnie manages to look cool. I wait as he changes from his uniform into his clothes in the bathroom. He seems agitated as we head outside and get in my car.

"Rumors are flying," he says grimly.

"You and Deena?" I ask, pulling out of the parking lot.

"No, that's a given."

"You guys back together?"

"Yeah."

"So what rumors?"

He looks at me with a small smile. I take my eyes off the road and gaze back at him. "Me?"

"Yup."

"Me and Marsha?" I guess this isn't surprising, considering we made out nonstop on the sofa the whole night.

"Nope."

Now I'm confused.

"Not who, Reed, what."

"What?" I repeat stupidly.

He leans back. "Apparently, Marsha Peterman is one satisfied babe."

"What?" I say again.

Hold on. *She* was the one who'd had a few drinks, not me. What's she been telling everybody? Does she think something happened that didn't? What does she think I did to her? All I did was kiss her!

Lonnie's grinning from ear to ear. He's stretching this out for as long as he can. I wish he'd come out with it, but I know one thing. It's gotta be okay. If it was serious or bad, he'd never string me along like this—he'd never torture me. So, I let him have his fun.

"Whenever you're ready, buddy, I'm all ears."

He keeps grinning.

"Anytime during this century."

Now he's laughing. He suddenly punches me in the shoulder, hard, but not for real.

"*Ooof,*" I yelp, not ready for it.

"You, sir, are a 'phenomenal kisser.' "

The double-yellow lines on the road blur in front of me. *Huh?*

He turns to face me. "You're a 'phenomenal kisser,' dude! Marsha's been telling the whole world how much she loved getting to know your talented mouth. She says you are—and I'm quoting the girl directly—'phenomenal.' "

"What are you talking about?" I demand.

He shakes his head. "I've been at this since third grade, Reed, you know that, and I've never gotten a rap like this." He shakes a fist at me. "Do you know how lucky you are? Kissing's the *golden goose!*" He punches me again, but not as hard. "You're a natural at this. You're a champ! It's, like, a hidden talent or something, waiting to come out, all these years. You know?"

I'm speechless. I'm actually good at something that has to do with girls?

Who knew?

Kissing Marsha was definitely awesome for me, but it never, ever occurred to me that it might be awesome for her too.

We reach the mall. Lonnie looks depressed as we exit the car. "You think you could give your old pal a few pointers on the Reed Technique?"

I burst out laughing. This is too much! Me? Instruct him?

"This is weird," I say. And it is.

Now Lonnie looks thoughtful. "Think about it, Reed. You did it by yourself. No tip list. No script. No textbook. No class. You did it. And, apparently, you've found your niche, my man. You could have a whole new career ahead of you. Reed Walton—Kissing Genius."

I laugh again. He's right—I did do it myself. And . . . somehow I managed to get it right. More than right!

"So what now?" I ask as we enter the mall.

"Practice makes perfect," Lonnie says, giving me a wink. "Start with Marsha, then conquer the world." He gets serious. "Are you seeing her again?"

"I don't know."

He looks confused. "I thought you liked her."

"Yeah, but . . ." I consider telling him, but change my mind. This is dangerous. We've never talked about it, and the truth is, I don't know how Lonnie would react to me telling him I have a huge thing for his sister.

Would he be okay with it?

Was it something he already suspected?

Would he beat me up?

"Who're you going to ask to the Fall Dance?" he asks, then whistles low. "You have your pick now!"

The Fall Dance is the first senior dance of the new semester. It's a big deal.

"I don't know."

"Marsha would go with you."

"Because of my kissing skills?"

He looks at me strangely. "What's going on, Reed?"

We pass the pet store. Before I can reply, I hear my name called. We both turn to see Rhonda Wharton waving at us.

Lonnie nods at me. "Later, dude."

"What—you're leaving?"

He looks at me like I'm a simpleton. "That's right, genius boy. You got company."

"But how will you get home?"

Now he looks positively nauseated. "You're killing me, buddy. Focus on the girl, will ya? I'll take a bus." He walks away, shaking his head at my maddening dorkliness.

Rhonda motions me over. I shuffle over to her, my mind reeling. We watch a bunch of brown puppies tumble over each other in the store window.

"Aren't they adorable?" she asks, scooting closer to me.

"Yeah," I mutter.

"Gives you the warm fuzzies, doesn't it?" she goes on, turning to face me.

"Yeah."

"Almost makes you want to kiss somebody, doesn't it?" she continues, tipping her face upward.

"Yeah."

"Maybe even the person next to you . . ."

"Yeah?"

I turn my head and Rhonda leans forward and kisses me. Just. Like. That.

My mouth knows what to do, but my brain's discombobulated.

My mouth is sending these signals: "Isn't this cool?"

My brain is responding with these signals: "What is the meaning of this? Need data! Cannot process!"

I can't believe this is happening. I'm kissing *another* girl. The next day! And it's Rhonda Wharton—a girl I've been drooling over since I was twelve—a girl I botched a previous kiss with. I'm getting a second chance. She practically attacked me!

Is this the way things are going to be from now on? Are girls going to grab me off the street and kiss me? Lonnie was right about kissing being the *golden goose*. Girls *adore* it. Is my luck changing—finally?

The kiss seems to last forever. Rhonda and I are all wrapped up in each other's arms—though I have no idea how we got that way—and it's awesome. Just like the kisses with Marsha. When it's finally over, Rhonda smiles and says, "Wow—Marsha was right!"

This makes me feel lousy. Maybe this isn't what I want, after all. Step right up to Marlborough's Official Kissing Booth? Kisses with Reed for a buck? I know a guy shouldn't complain about girls pulling him aside to test-drive his kissing expertise, but the more I think about it, the more I decide I don't want to be just a big walking mouth.

Rhonda must sense I'm having a problem with this, because she says softly, "I thought . . . I thought you wanted me to do that. I thought you liked me. I thought you always liked me. I guess not. I don't usually make out with boys in malls. I wouldn't have done that . . . It's not like . . ." Her eyes get misty.

For crying out loud!

I've gone from King of the Dorks to Heartbreak Hotel!

In one month!

"I like you," I say.

"You do?" She perks up.

"Um, yeah. It's just . . . well . . . the thing is . . ."

She bites her lip. "You don't like me."

I wish I could tell her the truth. I wish I could tell all these suddenly interested girls the truth:

Yes, Rhonda, you're right. I always liked you. When I was a freshman, I thought you were one of the most beautiful girls in school and I would've happily sold a kidney to do what we did now. But you wouldn't even look at me. You made me feel creepier than a cockroach.

So now that I've changed—even though I haven't—and acquired some weird sheen of hype and fame and coolness and kissability, you're suddenly into me? Where were you when I needed you? Why didn't you kiss me four years ago? Why didn't you kiss me last year? Why didn't you give me a chance until today?

"It's okay," she says quietly. "I just hoped . . . I know you want a girlfriend . . . I thought I could be . . ." She doesn't finish. Instead, she walks away. No, runs away.

I take a few steps in her direction, then change my mind. Her reaction makes me feel lower than something stuck to the bottom of someone's shoe, but I don't want to go after her. Rhonda's a dream girl, but, well, I'm too mixed-up right now to think straight.

Lonnie will string me up by my ankles for this.

I think about looking for him, but instead, I leave.

•   •   •

I'm not sure where I'm going. I'm gripping the steering wheel so tightly my knuckles are white. I find myself at the

Woodrow Wilson Basketball Courts at the George Washington Municipal Park. And the girl's there. I sit in the car and watch her.

"I don't even know you," I say out loud in the car. "But for some reason, I always end up here." I frown. "This drop-dead gorgeous girl, Rhonda, just stopped me in the mall to kiss me! I think she wants to be my girlfriend! Can you believe that? Me! It's crazy! We've had lockers next to each other since we were twelve, but if not for that, she wouldn't even know my name. I spent most of the last four years trying not to stare at her, but she barely looked my way the whole time. And then, a few weeks ago, she decides I'm okay, after all, and a few minutes ago, she jumps me in front of the pet store! Not that it wasn't totally incredible, but, I mean, what's going on? Are the planets aligned or something?"

I frown for the second time. "See, the thing is, I'm crazy about this girl I grew up with. She's amazing. She's always been my best friend—she's never made me feel bad about myself— even when I was overflowing with massive dork cooties. But she's got a boyfriend—a big, hairy, baboonlike boyfriend. She doesn't know how I feel about her and I'm too chicken to tell her, anyway."

I frown for the third time. "Before this year, I'd only asked out one girl in my entire life, Marsha, in my freshman year. I don't know why—I must have been postal." I shake my head, remembering. "I knew her class schedule by heart. I tried for five weeks to run into her, pretend I was in the hallway at the same time she was, and it finally happened between her

American Government and French classes, and somehow I managed to get it out, even though there was a hole burning in my stomach . . . and she laughed in my face.

"And now, Marsha's telling everybody how much she likes my kissing. I spent a whole night kissing her because she basically wouldn't let me stop. But none of these girls care that I existed before—except Ronnie. I was, like, a nobody for seventeen years, and all of a sudden, I'm a somebody." My eyes sting. "Why didn't anybody want to kiss me before now? I would've probably kissed the same way. Because I was a few inches shorter? Because I didn't have a car? Because I wore really thick glasses? Because I didn't have a Web site? How can things like that matter so much?"

I pause for a long time. "Ronnie's the one I want to be with." I stare down at my lap, then at the girl. "What do you think I should do?"

But the only reply I get is the sound of her ball pounding on the court. It seems to say:

"Reed—Reed—Reed—Reed."

"You're—killing—me."

. . .

When I get home, I find Mom in the kitchen, making a big pot of vegetable soup.

"Grandma's out with Leo," she sings. "Isn't that sweet? Just goes to show you there's never a wrong time for romance."

It must be my face, because Mom asks, "What's wrong, hon? What is it?"

"Nothing," I say automatically.

"Oh, Reed, something's wrong," she says. "Here, sit down."

I let her lead me to a chair at the kitchen table and she sits down next to me. I'm transported all of a sudden back to first grade, coming home from school, sitting in the kitchen with her, eating celery sticks slathered with peanut butter, telling her all about my day. I never spared a single detail—I even memorized the school lunch menu every day so I could report it back to her—and Mom always listened raptly and with absolute fascination, as if we were having the most riveting conversation in the world.

When did those days end? How come I stopped talking to her? Why didn't I tell her about my day anymore?

"What's the matter, sweetie?" she asks softly. "You look so sad."

"I'm not sad," I lie, looking away.

She waits a minute. "Well, all right," she finally says, getting up. "If you say so."

She doesn't say this with impatience and I know she's just giving me my space. Or maybe she's like my dad, using her therapist's skills to try and pull it out of me.

I don't say anything, but I don't get up either. I sit and watch her chop onions at the counter. Her eyes get all teary. She wipes them with a paper towel.

"Funny, isn't it? You'd think I was upset, if you didn't know about onions. I guess people can seem upset even when they're not."

I look away, then back. "Why is life so messed up?"

She's back at the table in two seconds flat. "Life, Reed? What's the matter? What's messed up?"

I hesitate. "Nothing," I finally mumble.

She waits. "All right, Reed, you know where to find me if you need me. Okay?"

"Okay," I say.

I sit there a little while longer, brooding, trying to decide whether I want to talk or not, then I give up and go to my room.

. . .

But Mom wastes no time in summoning the troops. Because when Grandma gets back from her date with Leo, the first thing she does is call me downstairs.

"I need your help, Reed, I'm desperate. I need a good pair of hands that know how to work with bread dough."

I play along. I roll up my sleeves and put up my hands for her inspection. "How are these?" I ask. "Will these do?"

She pretends to examine them. "You know, I think they're perfect."

We prepare a batch of rye bread dough and knead it side by side at the counter. Grandma has always liked me to help her with her baking. I'm sure I'm the only guy in school who can make pineapple upside-down cake from scratch.

Grandma observes my technique. "Oh, you're good, Reed, you're very good. When you were three years old, you know, you marched in here and demanded to learn how to bake. You wouldn't take no for an answer. You said, 'I'm going to be the world's best egg-cracker, Grandma.'"

I let out a laugh. "I said that?"

"Oh, yes," she replies. "You were a take-charge kind of three-year-old. Defeat wasn't in your vocabulary."

Huh. I was more cool when I was three years old than I am now.

Grandma seems to sense my feelings, because she goes on. "You're the same way now, you know, persistent and unbeatable. That's why you've done so well."

Grandma's right.

I've been pummeling myself nonstop, telling myself what a loser I am, but the truth really is . . . I Am Making Progress!

I mean, I kissed two girls in two days!

I'm a "phenomenal kisser"!

Girls *like* me. They *want* to kiss me.

I may have screwed up nonstop too—and I still don't have what I really want—but I'm getting there, slowly, painfully, in baby steps, *forward*, not backward.

By the time our fresh-baked rye bread comes out of the oven, I'm feeling better.

Things may not be all that great, but it's hard not to be happy when you're eating warm, homemade bread that you kneaded with your grandmother.

1. Would you kiss someone with beer breath?

HotStud: beer breath, coffee breath, dog turd breath, who cares?

greenfrog: if i had beer breath 2 lk when u both have curry

sk8erboy: if he was my bf yes but just some guy w/ beer breath no!

BabeHunter: guys make out w/ anybody w/ any kind of breath

TheDuke: if i was wasted

monster11: breath mints!

floweringgarlic: if it was reed! but i'm sure his breath would always be nice

DirtyGirl: if it was johnny depp

FallenAngel: stink-bomb beer breath? how bad we talking?

wicked: if ur going 2 a party where peeps are drinking beer they're going 2 have beer breath

2. What would you do if a guy asked you out like this: "Movie or dinner with me Saturday night"?

DirtyGirl: cute trick
monster11: dinner at best place in town!
greenfrog: both he he he
chiefcool: GR8 also pathetic
wicked: kewl
wrsssatty: movie so u don't have 2 talk
allstar: dinner so u can talk
floweringgarlic: amazing the lengths guys go 4 a d8. girls reject them 2 much

3. Should guys pay?

DirtyGirl: not every d8
greenfrog: the 1st time
sk8erboy: all the time
HotStud: what happened 2 feminism?
BabeHunter: guys should pay so when they're grabbing babes after they can say hey! I paid!
floweringgarlic: y does the poor guy have 2 go broke?
Mightyviking: seriously dating can get $$$$
LonerWolf: can't girls help out a little?

4. If a guy doesn't kiss you on your first date, what does that mean?

allstar: welcome splitsville population u
monster11: d'oh!
BabeHunter: he could be shy or scared or grossed out
el sexy: beer breath!
Mightyviking: ur toast
HotStud: guys are horndawgs. if a guy doesn't make out there's something seriously wrong lk alien fangs popping out & stuff

5. Should girls ask out guys?

DirtyGirl: woohoo!
sk8erboy: guys would lk that
HotStud: hello feminism? hello 21st century? hello equality? hello double standard? hello guys doin all the work?
allstar: I guess its ok
monster11: d'oh!
floweringgarlic: i don't but I'm not goin to tell other girls they can't
BabeHunter: babes ask me out. If they're hot i go out w/them if not don't. kapeesh?

And in the comments section:

DirtyGirl: did u pick marsha reed?
allstar: u & marsha lookd pretty happy at samantha's party

floweringgarlic: why didn't u pick me reed? i didn't have beer breath. i would've kissed u all nite long 2. you're a hottie! & i hear ur really nice.

HotStud: hey, reed, mind if i lap up all ur leftovers? ur just lookin 4 1 girl rite? why let all the babe-licious beauties go 2 waste? i'll give them good home. don't u worry.

The posts are even better this time. I feel like I'm getting to know everybody. HotStud's obviously demented, but everybody else is cool. Especially floweringgarlic. Who is she? Why does she like me so much? Do I know her?

"HotStud's pretty funny—in an extremely disturbed way," I say.

"Yeah," Ronnie replies absently.

We're on my Amish rug in front of my laptop, but Ronnie's staring blankly across the room.

"Is something wrong?" I ask her.

She shoots me a look of pure, uncensored revulsion. It totally startles me.

"Are you mad at me, Ronnie?" I ask. "What is it? What'd I do?"

What happens next is a time bomb. I set it off and it explodes in my face.

"Nobody's good enough for you, Reed!" Ronnie shouts, jumping to her feet. "Lonnie's been right all along—you're so *picky*!" She indicates my laptop. "I've been working my butt off to help you, and these girls are falling all over themselves to get to you, and you haven't contacted any of them!"

"Ronnie . . . ," I say, getting to my feet and reaching for her, but she whirls away from me.

"You were madly in love with Marsha Peterman for four years—and now she's begging you to go out with her! And Rhonda Wharton would go out with you in a minute! And they're not 'dogs' "—she wiggles her fingers to indicate quotation marks—"but you couldn't care less!"

"Ronnie . . . ," I say, reaching for her again, but this time she recoils from me as if I've hurt her.

"You said you wanted a girlfriend!" she goes on, and her voice breaks. "Well, I'm sorry none of us are brilliant like you! I'm sorry none of us are going to Princeton!"

"It's not that," I say desperately. "I swear, Ronnie, I don't care about that."

She puts her hands on her hips. "Well, what is it then, Reed?"

I swallow hard. "I . . . I like somebody else."

"Oh, *right*, Reed, your perfect mystery girl."

"She's not a mystery girl," I say quietly.

"Name her."

I look away.

"You're lying, Reed."

"No . . ."

"You think this is funny?"

"Ronnie, please . . ."

She sniffles. "You just don't care."

I throw my arms around her, but she breaks away with such ferocity it makes me take a step backward.

"You're doing this on purpose."

"No!"

She narrows her eyes at me. "For—the—last—time. Who is it?"

"It's . . . It's . . ."

Have you ever struggled to reach for something that's just out of range of your fingers? That's how I feel at that moment. I'm stretching myself as hard as possible to get to it, and I think I may almost have it in my grip, when Ronnie snarls, "I always thought it was because you were shy, Reed, but I was wrong." She pauses, then hisses, "You think you're better than everyone else."

"No," I whisper.

"I'm sick of you, Reed."

And she stomps out.

. . .

Is this what people have been thinking all this time? That I'm stuck up? Snobby? Better than them?

Talk about an image problem.

How can my best friend—a person I've known since I was five, a person I thought knew me better than anyone else— think that about me?

I feel like throwing up.

For the past hour, I've been sitting on the floor cradling my pounding head in my hands. I finally open my laptop.

ScreamingEagle: please don't be mad at me
ScreamingEagle: i'm sorry i'm such a dope

ScreamingEagle: i know how hard you've worked
ScreamingEagle: i know you're only trying to help me
ScreamingEagle: please talk to me
ScreamingEagle: i'm on my knees as i write this
ScreamingEagle: now I'm prostrate on the floor
ScreamingEagle: if i get any lower i'll be eating floor wax
ScreamingEagle: i beg you for forgiveness
ScreamingEagle: i throw myself at your mercy
ScreamingEagle: i don't think i'm better than you
ScreamingEagle: hello?
ScreamingEagle: anybody home?
ScreamingEagle: i thought my best friend lived here?
ScreamingEagle: ronnie?
ScreamingEagle: please don't give up on me

It's not working. She's ignoring me.

I take a deep breath. Then I type the thing I know will work.

ScreamingEagle: ill ask marsha to the fall dance tomorrow
FaerieCharmer: i'll believe it when i see it reed but i'll be the first to cheer

I stare at her words for a long time. I can't believe I've gotten Ronnie to talk to me by promising her I'd ask another girl to the dance.

I wish I had a clue how to make this work. I finally confess everything in an e-mail:

ronnie,

it's you. you're the mystery girl. you're the one i want
to take to the dance, you're the one i want to be with,
you're the one i want to kiss. please tell jonathan
(aka Magilla Gorilla) to play in parkway traffic and
give me a chance instead.

not better than you or anyone else,

reed

But I don't send it.

I do, however, save it in my DRAFTS folder.

. . .

Asking Marsha Peterman to the Fall Dance takes care of
itself.

Marsha takes matters into her own hands by cornering me
as I come out of AP Chemistry.

"I'm sorry about the beer breath thing on the Web site,
Marsha," I say, figuring that's why she's come to see me. "I'll
take it off."

"Oh, that's okay, I thought it was funny," she says.

What's this? Marsha Peterman being a good sport?

I start to move away, figuring I'll do the asking-to-the-
dance thing at the end of the day, but Marsha asks, "Reed, um,
are you going to the, um, Fall Dance?"

I stare at her. "Oh, well, actually, I'm glad you asked. . . ."

"You are?" she says, her face lighting up. "How come?
Because you want to . . . ask me?"

I open my mouth, then close it. She's completely knocked the wind out of my sails.

"Um, yeah," I say, figuring I'll make it formal for the record anyway. "Would you like to go with me?"

"Sure, Reed, I'd love to go with you," she answers, smiling. "I can't wait."

I remember asking her out when we were freshmen. It's been four years, but it feels like it happened an hour ago. I'll never forget her disgusted face, her cruel laugh, her indignant *"NO!"* As if I'd asked her to lick fresh boogers off the bottoms of my sneakers instead.

It wasn't just that Marsha rejected me. It was the ruthlessness of her rejection—the viciousness in her face and laugh and *"NO!"*—the sadism of it. It was the clear *pleasure* she took in crushing me—the obvious nerve she felt that a dork like me had dared to show, asking out a goddess like her.

Well, Marsha's face is completely different now—she's *thrilled* to be going to the Fall Dance with me—she practically asked me.

I can't believe I spent an entire night making out with her. A girl who sliced me to shreds. A girl I still wanted four years later. I wonder how Marsha would feel if I shot *her* down, if I laughed in *her* face, if I squashed *her* under my heel.

I realize I'm different, and not just on the outside. I'm not shuffling my feet, I'm not stuttering, my heart's not pounding in my ears, I'm not blabbering about coconut and trout like I did a month ago at her locker.

I'm different than I was four years ago.

I'm different than I was a month ago.

. . .

"I can't believe it," Lonnie says. "Wow."

We're in the school cafeteria and I've just told him about Marsha and the Fall Dance.

"That girl is hot for you."

I frown at that, and he catches it.

"Don't you like her?"

"Yeah," I say. "It's just . . . what she did to me four years ago."

"That was brutal," Lonnie says, nodding.

I'm grateful Lonnie understands this. I mean, I know four years is a pretty long time, and you're probably thinking I should be over it by now. But like most guys, Lonnie gets the concept of a guy carrying a scar-for-life, inflicted by a girl he loved.

I realize in that moment I'm lucky to have best friends of two genders. Ronnie wouldn't understand this Marsha-rejection thing as well as Lonnie. In fact, she'd probably call me a crybaby. (But she'd apologize right afterward.) Yet it's usually much easier to talk to Ronnie about this stuff than Lonnie.

Speaking of Ronnie, she's nowhere in sight, and I wonder if she's purposely avoiding me.

"Maybe you shouldn't have asked her," Lonnie says. "Maybe you should've said you'd think about it."

"I don't know," I say. "That's kind of cruel."

"Exactly."

"Nah," I say, shaking my head. "I couldn't do that to her."

"What about what she did to you, man?"

I think about it. "Maybe you're right. But it's too late now."

Lonnie seems thoughtful all of a sudden. "No, you're the one who's right, Reed. That's why you've got all these girls after you. You're a . . . nice guy."

I think he's teasing me about this, but Lonnie's serious. "Why do I spend so much time making sure I'm not?"

I don't know if he's addressing this question to me or himself, but I reply, "Not . . . a nice guy?"

"Yeah," he says, looking suddenly and totally morose.

I feel like I should give him a real answer. "I guess being nice is kind of . . . dorky," I venture. "Girls like . . . bad boys. So why shouldn't a guy make sure he's not too nice? You should just be yourself, Lonnie."

"I don't think I can," he answers softly. "I'm not even sure who I am."

"You'll figure it out," I say.

I realize this response is horribly inadequate, but I'm not sure what to say. I can't figure it out myself.

Ronnie suddenly plops down at the table, looking annoyed.

"Hey, Ronnie," I say nervously.

"Hey," she replies curtly.

My stomach twists up. "I asked . . . Marsha to the dance," I say, feeling very weird.

Ronnie studies me. "That's great, Reed. I'm glad you did."

Her words are friendly, but her tone isn't, and I wish I could confess everything right then and there. But I can't. The only thing I can manage is, "Will you give me dance lessons so I'm not a total doofus?"

Ronnie laughs. "Of course, Reed, anytime." She smiles at me, and even though I know there's still something guarded behind it, I feel better.

"Just don't give him any kissing lessons," Lonnie puts in. "He doesn't need those."

This hits way too close, but we all laugh.

Things have never felt more strange between the three of us.

. . .

The decorating committee does a good job at the Fall Dance. The school gym looks appropriately autumnlike—it's filled with pumpkins, hay bales, gourds, cornstalks, scarecrows, and chrysanthemums.

I arrive with Marsha Peterman clutching my arm in a death grip. She looks unbelievable. She's wearing a tiny orange dress that she says is a color called sienna. She says she bought it just for me. Me! All I know is it's practically painted on and my eyes keep drifting to it.

She's already lunged at me twice—once on her doorstep, once in my car. To be honest, I feel like I've stepped into an old sci-fi movie called *Invasion of the Body Snatchers*. The real Reed Walton—the poor, clueless, dorky kid who screws up nonstop with girls—is bound and gagged with strong duct tape in some broom closet somewhere. The guy passionately kissing Marsha Peterman—being lunged at by Marsha Peterman—is a slick impostor masquerading as me. How else to explain these astonishing changes?

I like kissing Marsha. But she isn't my first choice, of course. And yet, I can't help feeling that I've put myself in a very stupid, impossible situation. Here I've got this goddess whose idea of a good time is attaching herself to my face—and I'm not happy with it.

No wonder people like my parents have jobs. They'll never go out of business.

So what if Marsha treated me worse than dirt in my dork days? So what if she tortured me when I asked her out four years ago? And stomped away when I dared say "trout" in her presence a month ago? She isn't doing that now. She can't keep her hands off me. Maybe it's time to forgive her for her past sins against me. Maybe it's time to give her a second chance. After all, didn't I yearn for a night like this one? With her? As recently as a month ago?

Still, I can't help scanning the crowd for Ronnie as Marsha and I dance to the first slow song of the evening. I must stare across the room for too long, because Marsha promptly pulls my head down for another kiss-a-thon.

The girl's a make-out addict! Not that I'm complaining. But who knew I'd be her drug of choice?

I spot Ronnie at last and she spots me, and I realize she's probably witnessed every detail of my furious lip-lock with Marsha. I feel confused and confounded.

Lonnie and Deena edge up to us.

"How's it goin'?" Lonnie asks with a wink.

Deena and Marsha giggle like crazy.

"Time to powder our noses," Deena whispers to Marsha in some mysterious girlspeak I don't understand. They head off to the bathroom.

"You're a kissing fiend," Lonnie says after they've gone.

I clear my throat. "She's like a leech."

"I feel for you," he says. "Mouth getting a tough workout and all."

"I'm not complaining," I say.

"Good, 'cause I'll knock out your genius brains if you do."

We decide to get something to drink. On the way to the refreshments, we pass a bunch of girls. Lonnie wanders off to look for ice. I pour myself some soda and inadvertently over-hear their conversation. I guess they can't see me because of the giant potted palms between us.

Girl #1: You're so lucky, Marsha, snagging that hottie, Reed.

Marsha (giggling): I know. He's amazing.

Girl #2: Is he really a phenomenal kisser?

Marsha (in a serious tone): He is, like, the best ever. He's some kind of genius. If only I'd known earlier . . .

My ears actually ring.

Girls talking about me? And the stuff they're saying?

It's unreal. It's *history*.

But I wonder. Would Marsha really have gone out with me earlier if she knew about my kissing talents? I doubt it. I don't believe for a second she would have gone out with me when I was a Card-Carrying Dork—no matter how skilled I was in the kissing department. Maybe she just likes the whole new package she's getting now.

On the other hand, I really shouldn't talk. I mean, would I have asked her out in the first place if she weren't so cute? Would I be with her now? The truth, I realize, is that I'm no better than she is. All this time, I thought I was somehow nobler, but I'm not. I'm as shallow as everybody else.

Lonnie returns with the ice, saving me from too much heavy brain lifting.

"You're going to need a tip list tonight, Reed. *How to Be with a Girl Who's Boiling-White-Hot for You.*"

I spit out my soda.

Lonnie pats my back. "Chill, Reed. I was kidding. You won't need a tip list."

Why'd he have to go and bring this up? I may be okay at kissing, but I don't know how to do anything else, and now I'll be dealing with it all night long. He must sense my panic, because he tries to make a joke.

"It's cool, Reed, just tell her you have a headache."

I smile feebly. From across the room, Rhonda Wharton approaches the refreshments. Lonnie goes off to find something to eat.

"Hey, Rhonda," I say, still feeling funny about what happened at the mall.

"Hey," she says softly, giving me a small smile.

I grasp for safe topics to bring up. I can't think of anything. Maybe I should leave. Instead, I ask, "Are you here with anyone?"

"Myself."

"Oh." This makes me feel odd, even though it has nothing to do with me. Right?

"Would you . . . like to dance?"

I don't know why I ask her this. Maybe because I feel bad. Or maybe because I want to dance with her. Or maybe because I want to give her a chance to turn me down. To even things out between us.

But she nods. I take her hand and lead her to the dance floor.

Once we're there, she asks me, "Are you and Marsha . . . going together?"

"I don't think so," I stammer. "Not really."

How lame! But I guess I don't really know. I didn't think so until this point, but what does Marsha think? When you kiss a girl that much, does that mean you're going with her? Is it wrong of me to kiss her like that and not go out with her?

Rhonda's face brightens. She doesn't say anything else, but she doesn't have to. It's pretty obvious, even to me. I want to shake my head. Girls fighting over me. Gorgeous goddess girls fighting over me!

Me!

Unreal.

When I get back home tonight, I'm going to look for the gagged and bound version of myself in all the closets in the house. 'Cause the guy at the Fall Dance sure isn't anyone I know.

When Marsha spots me dancing with Rhonda, she glides over and doesn't just butt in, but takes my face in her hands and plants the mother, father, grandmother, and grandfather of all lip-locks on me. I don't resist, argue, or go after Rhonda. I am, after all, technically here with Marsha, who is obviously more territorial than a saber-toothed tiger. In fact, I feel like I should have a giant *M* branded on my forehead:

Marsha Peterman—Property Of.
Make-Out Marathon Currently in Progress—Please Do
   Not Disturb.
Mine! Keep Your Hands Off!

I'm flattered, really. Isn't this what I've always wanted? Dreamed of? Craved?
Besides, what difference does it make?
Marsha.
Rhonda.
The person I really want to dance with is being manhandled on the dance floor by a dumb, furry primate. I look in Ronnie's direction, but Marsha turns my head and gives it to me again. The girl's got inner radar about this stuff!

At midnight, a bunch of us decide to go to the Marlborough Diner for breakfast. It makes as much sense as anything else. I go to the coatroom to get our stuff. That's when I hear crying. I part a row of coats and find Ronnie curled up in a ball on the floor.

"Ronnie? What are you doing here? What's wrong? Where's Jonathan?"

I lower myself next to her and she puts her arms around me and asks in a shaky voice, "Can you take me home, Reed?"

"Of course," I say softly. "Here—give me your cell." I'm probably the only guy in the Northern Hemisphere without a cell phone.

I call Lonnie on Ronnie's cell, even though he's right in the next room.

"Yo," he answers on the third ring.

"It's Reed. Listen. Can you tell Marsha I had to go? Can you take her home for me? Can you tell her I'm really sorry? I'll explain later."

He's silent for a long time. "Are you okay? Is everything okay? Where's Ronnie?"

"She's fine. I'm fine. She's with me. I'll explain tomorrow. Okay?"

He hesitates. "Okay," he finally says.

I hang up and help Ronnie to my car. She's limp and lethargic. Her eyes are bloodshot. I want to know what happened to her. But I know I shouldn't push it. She's upset enough as it is. If she wants to tell me, she will.

When we arrive at her house, I walk her to the front door. She asks me to come inside, so I do. The house is dark and quiet. There's only a dim lamp on in the living room. She flings herself onto the sofa. I sit down next to her.

"Jonathan broke up with me," she says.

I gather her into my arms and she rests her head on my chest. "You're better off without him. You were too good for him."

She starts to cry.

I realize that's probably not what she wanted to hear. After all, she and Jonathan were together a long time. She really liked him. What she probably wants me to say is, I'm sure he'll call tomorrow to apologize, I'm sure they'll get back together, I'm sure this is nothing. After all, Ronnie broke up with him a zillion times, but they always got back together.

But I don't want to say those things. What I want to say is I'd be the best boyfriend in the world if she'd give me a chance instead of him.

She hiccups. "Oh, Reed, I'm so sorry I yelled at you the other day. You didn't deserve that. And I'm also sorry I forced you to do this *Girlfriend Project*. I hope you can forgive me. You're such a great friend. You've always been such a great friend."

I hug her close. I kiss her hair, her neck, her cheek. Then I stop. She's broken up with her boyfriend and is obviously unhappy about it, she just told me what a great friend I am, and here I am pawing her.

She stares at me for ages. Then she kisses me on the mouth, just once, soft and sweet. I close my eyes with a sigh, wishing for more, but knowing what I want will probably never happen.

But I'm wrong. She kisses me again, and even though I can hardly believe it, the next thing I know, we're making out like crazy.

It's fantastic. I have one arm around her waist and the other threaded through her hair, and I feel filled up with the scent of her, the feel of her. I'm having trouble breathing. Her arms are around my neck, her hands twirling the hair at the back of my head, something she's always done, something I've always liked, except now we're kissing while she's doing that. We're kissing!

She finally pulls away and I brace myself for the inevitable: It was a mistake, she got carried away, it's time for me to go now, thanks for the ride home, she won't tell Jonathan about this, have a nice life.

Instead, she says with a sly smile, "So the rumors were true."

I start to smile, then stop. Is *that* what this is? Yet another test-drive? Like Rhonda at the mall? Ronnie stepping up to the Kissing Booth?

I'm so ticked off I can barely think straight. I'm about to get up, but Ronnie says, "We should've done that a long time ago, Reed."

What?

"I'm a yutz," she goes on. "I'm the mystery girl, aren't I?"

I nod slowly.

She rubs her nose against mine. "Well, mister, we've got a lot of catching up to do."

I smile. "I'm here for you anytime, Ronnie, you know that. Just say when."

"When."

I kiss her again, and again, and again.

. . .

I'm on her doorstep the next morning with a bouquet of yellow roses. I hope what happened last night wasn't a figment of my imagination, but I brace myself again for the inevitable. I know these things have a tendency to wilt in daylight.

But when she sees me at the door, she jumps into my arms and gives me a slow, sweet kiss that leaves me breathless.

"Oh, Reed," she sighs. "You're incredible."

I grin. "Can I take you out for breakfast?"

She laughs. "Why not?"

How perfect is this?

I've got the girl next door.

. . .

We decide to go to the Perkins in Hazlet, a few towns over, instead of the IHOP in town or the Marlborough Diner. Things feel very secretive.

Ronnie shoots me nonstop glances of delight as we drive over. "So, you always liked me, Reed?"

I smile at her. "Pretty much since kindergarten."

"Why didn't you ever tell me?"

This line of questioning makes me uncomfortable. "I thought you'd crush me like a grape, Ronnie."

"What? Why would I do that?"

"Because I wasn't the 'better specimen' I am now," I say, throwing her words back at her.

"Reed! I didn't mean any of that applied to me!"

"Honestly, Ronnie? If I'd told you last year? The year before? When I was a freshman? When I was a full-fledged Dork of the Lowest Order?"

"Reed! I would've done the same thing I did last night— jumped you. You've always been a great guy—freshman year, sixth grade, third grade. Have I ever treated you differently? Do I treat you differently now?"

"Well, you did kiss me. Quite extensively. Last night. Remember? On the sofa in your living room."

She grins. "Because you kissed me quite extensively."

I shake my head. "I don't know."

"Why don't you believe me?"

"Because all the evidence is to the contrary."

"You mean because of Marsha and Rhonda and all that?"

"Yeah, all that," I say. "Maybe this is a survey question for the site."

Her eyes widen. "You don't want me to shut down the site?"

I turn to her. "I want you to do whatever you want. As long as you replace Jonathan with me."

She laughs. "Done."

We're quiet for a little while.

135

"What about Lonnie?" I ask at last.

She looks at me. "What about him?"

"He's your brother."

"You think?"

I smile, but ask seriously, "Is he going to beat me up?"

"Maybe. What about Marsha?"

"What about her?" I ask.

"Is she going to beat *me* up?"

"Definitely," I reply with a laugh.

She sighs. "You're leaving behind a long trail of broken hearts, you know."

"I can't believe that," I murmur. "I can't believe any of this."

If someone had told me last summer that girls like Marsha Peterman, Rhonda Wharton, and Ronnie White would be clawing one another to get me, I'd tell them they were smoking some mean banana peels.

"Reed, when are you going to *get it*?" she asks impatiently. "Your brain's so full of calculus and chemistry and biology there's no room for common sense! You—are—a—great—guy. How many times do I have to tell you that? I swear I'm going to pull my hair out! Then I'm going to pull your hair out!"

I frown. "Marsha Peterman didn't think I was a great guy." This sounds bitter and whiny, but I don't care.

"Marsha Peterman is one girl!" Ronnie yells. "And, I might add, in case you haven't noticed, this same Marsha Peterman is desperately in love with you now."

"Desperately in love with my mouth, maybe."

Ronnie sighs again. "How many girls did you ask out before *The Girlfriend Project*? In all your years of high school?"

"One."

"And that was?"

"Marsha Peterman."

"I rest my case."

We reach the restaurant and I park the car.

Ronnie says, "Maybe, if you'd asked out other girls, you'd have an argument. But you didn't, so I suggest you shut up and kiss me. And don't stop till I tell you to. I want some serious lip action from the world's greatest kisser and I want it now."

I lean over and do as I'm told.

. . .

We drive down the Shore after breakfast. In New Jersey, you don't go to the beach or the ocean. You go "down the Shore." Not "to the Shore." And when you get there, you're not "at the Shore," you're still "down the Shore."

Everything on the boardwalk in Belmar is closed except for a greasy dive selling vinegar fries, so we buy a bucket and walk along the beach, listening to the crash of the surf, fending off insane seagulls wanting a free handout, and kissing like crazy. The kiss-a-thon between Marsha and me was nothing compared to the one between me and Ronnie. We are *totally* catching up.

"I wish you'd kissed me earlier, Reed," Ronnie says, pulling me down to the sand.

"I'm glad you like it," I whisper.

"You are so great, Reed," she sighs. "But you don't think you are. You're like New Jersey—like that contest your grandmother's trying to win. But, then, you've always been the Ultimate Jersey Guy."

I lift up my head in surprise. "Are you a mind reader or something? Did you have a microchip implanted in my brain?"

"It's my brain," she says, placing her hands on my head. "Everything—all of this—is mine, mine, mine."

"Yours, yours, yours," I say.

We roll around the sand like those people in that famous movie *From Here to Eternity*, except we don't get so close to the water that we get wet. I wonder if we'll be arrested, but I really don't care. I wish someone would pinch me. This can't be happening. It's too good to be true.

When we finally get back in the afternoon, Lonnie's sitting on his stoop looking extremely pissed off.

"Where have you guys been?" he asks, exactly like a parent would. "I wake up and it's like the day after the apocalypse. There's nobody around, I'm all by myself, nobody cares. Where'd you go? Couldn't you wait for me?"

He seems so forlorn, so lost, so *upset*. I feel terrible.

"Chill, Lonnie," Ronnie says gently, putting a hand on his shoulder. "I'm sorry we left like that. I'll make you a great big sandwich oozing with ketchup, okay?" She bends down next to him. "Come on, big guy, give me a smile."

He pretends to be annoyed, but says grudgingly, "Okay, but cut the crusts off."

I let out a laugh and he looks at me sheepishly. Ronnie grins and goes in the house.

It's time to face the music.

I'm a dead man. I have no chance at all.

The best thing to do is let him knock me out with one punch, then pretend I'm dead, like you're supposed to do when you meet a bear in the woods.

"What happened last night?" he suddenly asks. "Marsha was, like, a train wreck. I thought she was gonna fling herself into the nearest body of water. What did you do to that girl, Reed? Did you slip some love potion number 9 into her Diet Coke when she wasn't looking? She is, like, *nutters* for you!"

This distracts me. Marsha—*nutters* for me? Have things changed or what?

"I hope you called her," Lonnie goes on. "Because, if you didn't, she's probably filled up your whole machine by now." He shakes his head. "Man, Reed, overnight you've become the player of the year."

I don't know what to say. It's more shocking to me than anyone.

He peers at me. "So what happened?"

I take a deep breath. "Jonathan broke up with Ronnie."

His fists clench, and it makes me take a step back. I can't help it.

"She asked me to take her home," I continue, a little more shakily. "That's why I had to leave."

"Always hated that hairy guy's guts," Lonnie growls. "I'm glad things are over. Was she okay?"

"Yeah, but . . . something else happened."

He waits.

I cough. "Actually, I don't know how to tell you. I'm freaked out about it. Just remember this: You're bigger than me, we've been best friends for over ten years, and I'll miss my AP exams if you put me in the hospital. I was hoping to place out of the foreign language requirement."

"What are you talking about?" he roars. "Are you on acid?"

"I kissed your sister," I say with resignation. "I have a thing for her. I've always had a thing for her. We're going together."

He blinks. "You kissed Ronnie?"

"Yeah. Look, just hit me, okay? I can't stand the waiting. Let's get it over with."

He laughs. "I am vastly insulted, my friend. We may live in Jersey, but not everybody in the Garden State is a hitman. Next you'll be asking me to say 'youse guys' and 'fuggedaboutit'!"

"So, you're . . . okay with this?"

"Well . . ." Lonnie gives me a funny look. "Ronnie can be . . . I mean . . . She's . . ."

"What?" I ask sharply.

"She breaks up with guys, Reed. A lot."

"I know," I say defensively. That's true. "But I'm the *right* guy." That's true too.

Lonnie knits his brows together. "Yeah, well, I guess Ronnie can kiss anybody she wants. Sometimes I gotta wonder about her taste. . . ."

Ronnie comes bounding out of the house with a towering sandwich teetering on a paper plate. She pulls us both into a big hug.

"We're one happy tribe here. What more could a girl want out of life than two great guys by her side?"

She gives each of us a soft kiss—Lonnie on the cheek, me on the mouth.

Lonnie's right about Marsha. There are four telephone mes-
sages, five e-mails, and six text-messages.

The girl's having a meltdown!

All I did was take her to one dance—I didn't think we were
going together or anything—and she's losing it. Still, I decide
the right thing to do is talk to her in person. I call and ask her if
I can come over. She's thrilled beyond belief to hear from me.
As I drive over, I think of tip lists for this situation:

- How to Break Up with a Girl Who You Weren't Going Out
  with in the First Place
- How to Break Up with a Girl Who's Addicted to Your
  Kisses
- How to Break Up with a Girl Who Laughed in Your Face and
  Smashed Your Heart to Smithereens Four Years Ago, but

You Still Pined for Her, Took Her to a Dance, and Kissed Her till Your Lips Went Numb

But I don't feel like I need any tip lists.

This isn't a happy situation for me or Marsha. But I feel, well, if not confidence, then, at the very least, a lack of freaking-out-ness.

When I get to her house, the first thing Marsha does is lunge at me. Only this time, I stop her before she has a chance to kiss me, and realize this is the first time I've ever done such a thing in my entire life. Frankly, it blows my mind. Not only is a girl jumping me, but I'm stopping a girl from jumping me, because I've got *another* girl jumping me.

Reed Walton? Come in, Reed Walton!

Who *is* this dude impersonating you anyway?

Marsha bites her lip and looks like she's about to cry. I feel awful about it.

"I'm sorry, Marsha," I say softly. "I . . . I have to talk to you."

We sit on the sofa in her living room. Before I can start, though, she says, "I know I wasn't nice to you before, Reed, but I really like you now. Can't you . . . give me a second chance? Please?"

I'm thunderstruck. When I don't answer, she says, "I want, I want . . . to be your girlfriend. Isn't that what you want? A girlfriend?" She looks down, then back up. "I . . . I thought you liked me."

"You tortured me," I say.

I don't mean this to come out like an accusation. I just can't believe what I'm hearing. But it sends Marsha into some kind of tailspin.

"I'm sorry!" she exclaims. "Can't we start over? Won't you ever forget it? Can't I have another chance? Do I have to beg? It was four years ago!"

"It's just . . . I can't help it," I say. "It's . . . tattooed on my brain. You were repulsed by me . . . now you like me. I don't get it."

She looks down at her lap. "Well, I'm not gonna lie to you, Reed. You've changed. I mean, you've got to know that. I know it makes me sound superficial and everything to say that." She shifts uncomfortably. "But, then, you haven't changed at all, Reed. You were always a nice guy. You were nice to me at Samantha's party—you didn't have to be. You were nice to me at the Fall Dance, even though I treated you like a kind of possession or something." She gives me a small smile. "And if I had any sense at all, I wouldn't have done that to you four years ago. I would've gone out with you." She gazes at me. "Then I might have you now, and we wouldn't be having this discussion. We'd be kissing instead, which, of course, is a whole other thing." She grins. "You're such a great kisser, Reed. You're the best kisser of all the boys I've kissed." She gives me a shy look. "I love kissing you."

Now I'm *really* thunderstruck. And hot. My whole body feels like it's roasting over a barbecue grill.

"I wish we could start over too," I say quietly. "I had a crush on you for four years."

She seems very pleased with that.

"But . . . I like someone else now. We just started going together."

Her lower lip trembles.

And it occurs to me no matter what side of the line you're standing on—the one doing the rejecting or the one being rejected—it's not a nice place to be.

I'm not happy about doing this to Marsha. But if I was honest with myself, I'd admit a part of me wanted it to happen. A part of me thirsted for revenge on her. A part of me wanted this exact thing to occur.

But a bigger part of me doesn't want it to happen. A bigger part of me wishes I didn't have to do it at all.

Even when you're not cruel and sadistic—like Marsha was to me four years ago—even when you do it nicely, gently, even when you say all the right things, you feel awful about rejecting someone just the same.

"Who is she?" Marsha asks shakily.

"Ronnie."

She sniffles. "She's so lucky, Reed."

. . .

My breakup experience with Marsha blows every single fuse in my brain, causing a massive power outage in every cerebral circuit.

Marsha started bawling her eyes out when I got up to go. I sat back down immediately. I couldn't leave her crying like that. I couldn't be so heartless—even if I wanted to be, even if she deserved it.

So I held her, let her sob into my shoulder, stroked her hair. She tried to kiss me twice, but I drew the line there. Marsha's persistent—I'll give her that.

When I left at last, Marsha thanked me for staying with her a little longer. She said we could be friends. I bent down and kissed her on the cheek. I don't know why. It just seemed like a nice thing to do. She told me I was a "really decent guy." She seemed sincere about it too.

My wires are overloaded. I can't believe I made Marsha Peterman cry.

Over me!

Mastering organic chemistry at Princeton will be easier than this stuff.

What it comes down to, I think, is this:

Exhibit A: Reed Walton, formerly a lower-order dork-serf, currently a clever parasite invading the body-host of a hot stud (!) and kissing bandit-savant (!), comforting a girl who once crushed *him*, because, apparently, he's just crushed *her*?

Exhibit B: Marsha Peterman, formerly a goddess, currently a goddess (pretty much always a goddess), a girl who could have anybody—except the one guy she can't—please see above—whom she could've enslaved for eternity four years ago.

I would've been Marsha's slave-for-life if she'd said yes to me four years ago. But now I was turning *her* down—and there was nothing fun about it. And yet, I was comforting a girl who'd messed me up so badly I'd never asked out anyone else!

You don't need to tell me how weird my life has become.

Ronnie told me she would've gone out with me earlier if I'd asked her. But Marsha admitted the reason she liked me now was because I'd changed.

Maybe it does depend on the girl. Maybe Ronnie's right about that.

Marsha obviously cared about the way I looked. Well, what's so surprising about that? Don't I care about that too when it comes to girls? Don't most people care about it?

But what about other girls? If I'd asked out other girls, not just Marsha, would they have cared as much?

Would they have said yes?

After all this time, was the real issue, in fact, not that I was a *Dorkus Extremus*, but that I hadn't asked out enough girls?

I'd only asked out Marsha.

I'd asked out *one girl*.

Still, I ran into rotten luck! I mean, why did the first girl I ever ask out in my life have to be Marsha? Why did I make such a bad choice? Why did I lean toward someone who would traumatize me—only to resurface four years later as my biggest fan? And is it the universe's idea of a practical joke to have Marsha practically beg me to be her boyfriend now?

Most importantly, why did I give up so easily?

Marsha turning me down freshman year set the tone for the rest of high school.

I pretended grades were more important than girls. I pretended my student life was more important than my love life.

I had an identity problem.

I had an image problem.

And I gave up.

Why was I so lame? Why didn't I just *try again*?

Because I convinced myself I was a loser. Well, maybe I was, and maybe I would've been shot down by other girls again, again, again, and again.

But maybe not.

I'll never know.

A feeling of deep depression washes over me.

All the wasted time, all the wasted opportunities, all the Saturday nights I could've been out!

All the kissing I could've done!

I could've had a better four years than I did.

It was my own fault. I was scared of my own shadow.

I decide if I've learned anything from all this, it's this:

Letting Fear Rule Your Life Is Stupid.

. . .

1. Has anyone ever laughed at you after you asked them out? If yes, did you *not* ask out anybody else because you were so hurt? How long did your hurt last?
2. Have *you* ever rejected anyone? How did that feel?

3. How important are looks to you?
4. Have you ever liked someone and not told them? For how long?
5. Are you afraid of the opposite sex?

I write the questions myself when I get home. This site may have started as a publicity gag, but now, I need to conduct serious research.

Maybe I can help other people avoid making the same mistakes I did.

"Being a guy is hard work," Lonnie says.

"Tell me about it," I mumble.

"Well, at least we don't have to wear pantyhose."

"Or mascara," I say.

"We don't get periods."

"Or PMS," I add.

We're in my room discussing the questions I put on the site. Lonnie's and my both having a sister definitely gives us a bigger window into girlhood than most guys have. Not that it's done much for me. Or, surprisingly, *him*.

"You'd think I'd be better at this," Lonnie says.

"I don't get it, Lonnie," I say. "All I hear from you lately is how bad you are at this."

He pauses for a second, then replies, "It's all just an act. Reed. Don't you know that?"

Well, yeah, I knew that. "But why are you admitting it now? After all this time? Why all of a sudden?"

"I don't know," he murmurs, then turns to me. "Maybe because of you. *The Girlfriend Project*. Comparing myself."

"Comparing yourself? To me?"

"Yup."

"*Me?*"

"Reed, enough already. You're *good*. And you did it without an act. You didn't change. Well, maybe, a little. But you never pretended."

I don't know what to say to this. "I don't know who I am at all," I stammer. "I just found out people might think I'm stuck up. I'm trying to figure it out too."

"Join the club, dude."

"I feel like I wasted the last four years," I go on.

He shrugs. "Maybe you did, Reed, but you're catching up quick."

"Maybe . . . It's sort of like that contest," I venture.

"What contest?"

"You know, the state motto contest. New Jersey: We Have an Image Problem and, Thanks, We Know That."

Lonnie grins. "New Jersey: Jersey Guys May Be Messed Up but They're Hot."

"And They're Great Kissers Even Though They Don't Know What They're Doing Half the Time," I reply.

"And They're Hot."

"And They're Sensitive Guys."

"And They're Hot."

"And They Love Big Hair."

"And They're Hot."

We both crack up. Lonnie checks his watch. "Hey, we better get going."

We're going on a double date. Lonnie and Deena, Ronnie and me.

I'm still not sure how to act around Lonnie with Ronnie. It's stranger than I thought it would be, and sometimes I wonder . . . But then I remind myself that Ronnie and I are perfect for each other.

We go to this cool restaurant in Red Bank called the Melting Pot, where you order food and dip it into a collective fondue pot on your table. Ronnie keeps feeding me chunks of Italian bread dipped in cheese sauce, and I keep staring at Lonnie to make sure he's not freaked about it.

"You two are so cute it makes me want to hurl," Deena says cheerfully. She turns to Lonnie. "Are we that cute?"

"You're the cutest of them all," he replies—wisely.

She giggles. Then she looks at us again.

"So, you guys were best friends your whole lives, and now you're together. That is so cool. Can boys and girls stay friends or will they always get together in the end?"

"Survey question," Ronnie and I say together.

Deena laughs. "Yeah, what's happened with your site, Reed, is unbelievable. Everybody knows you. Everybody loves you."

I've actually been thinking about this. "They don't really know me," I say. "They like me because I'm famous. You shouldn't like someone just because they're famous. That's why people like celebrities. It's messed up."

"Yeah," Deena says listlessly.

"It's like when Floyd Flavin got arrested," I go on, undeterred. "I mean, the guy got arrested! Isn't that supposed to be a bad thing? Instead, it made him the most popular guy in school." I shove a hunk of cheese-soaked bread into my mouth and tell myself to shut up. My pious Boy Scout virtues are showing. It's okay for me to say these things when I'm with Ronnie and Lonnie. They understand me. But Deena isn't exactly safe territory.

"I don't know," Deena mutters.

I look at her and think, Man, this girl is an *airhead*. Then I scold myself for my meanness. But it's true. Deena Winters is so beautiful she belongs on the cover of a magazine. But she's a few enchiladas short of a combination platter, if you know what I mean. And yet, Lonnie's not an airhead at all. What does he see in her except the obvious? I guess that's enough for him.

I tell myself to stop thinking unkind thoughts about other people. Who am I to make judgments like that? Maybe Deena Winters saved somebody's life once. Maybe she rescues animals. Maybe she volunteers at a children's hospital every Sunday. Maybe she doesn't step on worms when they come out after it rains. I want to apologize to her for my rudeness, but at least I didn't insult her out loud.

Instead, I gaze appreciatively at Ronnie. She's beautiful and sweet and smart. I lean forward and kiss her softly, unable to help myself, and she smiles at me. Then I automatically look at Lonnie for his approval.

He's studying me with an expression I recognize.

It shocks me.

He's jealous.

. . .

All my life I wished I could be more like Lonnie.

But now, I realize, it's *hard* for Lonnie to be Lonnie. It's much harder for him than I ever knew.

When our double date's over and we're back in my room, Lonnie asks me, "Is this what you meant all along, Reed?"

I'm sitting in a chair by the window and Ronnie's down the hall in the bathroom.

"Yeah," I say, knowing exactly what he's asking. "This is it."

"I'm jealous."

"I know."

"So, this is what you meant by 'love' coming into the picture," he says, falling backward onto my bed.

"You shouldn't be jealous of me, Lonnie," I say. "I'm still a dork and I always will be. You're *It*."

"You're not a dork," he says. "And, even if you are, at least you're a happy one. You figured it out. I'm a restless caveman. I kiss anything that breathes."

I chuckle. "Well, you do have your reputation."

He gives me a small smile. "You got the better deal, buddy."

"Doesn't mean you can't get it too."

He rubs his face. "Can you write it up for me in a tip list?"

I laugh, and he does too.

He suddenly sits up. "New Jersey," he says, "Pass the Pepperoni and Quit Worrying About What Other People Think."

"New Jersey," I say, "We May Have Our Problems, but Get Out of Our Face."

"New Jersey," Ronnie says, entering the room, "Jersey Guys Are the Hottest and the Coolest."

"And They're Fantastic Kissers," I add with a grin.

"And They're the Hottest," Lonnie puts in.

"And They're the Coolest," Ronnie finishes.

. . .

1. Has anyone ever laughed at you after you asked them out? If yes, did you *not* ask out anybody else because you were so hurt? How long did your hurt last?

Mightyviking: yea 3 yrs

BabeHunter: it hurts worse than being kicked u-know-where

LonerWolf: ya ya 2 yrs & counting

FlavorOfTheMonth: i askd out a guy once. it was so hard. i can c why guys get freaked abut it

wicked: who needs the aggravation? i'm better off playin *war craft*

HotStud: i was majorly bummd 4 a month. Thanks 4 bringing up a painful memory 4 me reed

DirtyGirl: such a sad question 2TM!

RBJ: she laughed so hard it was lk i told a joke. i guess i was the joke.

allstart: OMG! i laughed at someone by accident! i didn't mean it! now i feel horrible! what should i do?

el sexy: i still haven't asked out anyone else

sykotic: no one laughs. maybe i'm lucky

TheDuke: she didn't laugh but she hung up

Grrl: i asked out a guy and he said no. i'm not doing it again

2. Have *you* ever rejected anyone? How did that feel?

FlavorOfTheMonth: not fun at all

BabeHunter: some guys think its kewl but they're sick puppies

sk8erboy: it sucked

SoldierOfFortune: hurts less than me being rejected

allstar: the guys u lk r the 1s who reject u & the guys u don't lk are the ones u reject. why?

el sexy: i think i would like it!

floweringgarlic: be careful who u reject. the "dork" of today cud be the hunk of tomorrow. & dont think he'll forget what u did to him.

chiefcool: i felt lk dog turd the drippy mushy kind.

3. How important are looks to you?

MobsterMo: very but not proud of it

el sexy: shallow but still important

floweringgarlic: don't judge a book by its cover

Mightyviking: that's the way things are even in those tribes in the amazon rain forest

BabeHunter: guys r no better than chimps

sk8erboy: it's biology. my dad is a biologist. it's chemistry

greenfrog: 2 bad wen ur fat or ugly

allstar: girls r more into guys having hot cars or $$$$ or both

FlavorOfTheMonth: if girls like bad boys it's all about hotness

DirtyGirl: it's more important to have a good personality and sense of humor

HotStud: ofc looks r important. what do you think nose jobs and wonderbras and zit concealer r for?

4. Have you ever liked someone and not told them? For how long?

monster11: a whole yr

wicked: i told her after 2 yrs & she told me 2 get lost

sk8erboy: i had a crush on my statistics teacher for the longest time but i never told him

el sexy: i lk this girl at the video store but she has a stupid gorilla-bf

floweringgarlic: i know boys who secretly like a girl for years and never tell her! what's the point? just tell her! maybe she likes u too!

cranialtornado45: so much wasted luv

greenfrog: my best friend likes this guy in gym & i don't think she'll ever tell him

allstar: i liked a guy at summer camp but didn't tell him till the last day and he liked me too and that was really stupid because we could have been together

HotStud: if i like a girl i tell her. why deprive her of the best time of her life?

5. Are you afraid of the opposite sex?

wrsssatty: OFC

DirtyGirl: guys are terrified of girls which is really sad. why are the questions so sad this time?

chiefcool: girls are man-eating blood-sucking fang-toothed cobra-headed monsters who toy w/guys for sport!

BabeHunter: they play games w/ur mind

el sexy: i'm afraid of poisonous snakes. any connection?

floweringgarlic: boys and girls misunderstand each other too much. we don't speak the same language sometimes

allstar: i feel afraid when i'm around a guy. my heart beats fast and my stomach gets crampd

HotStud: what's to be afraid of? girls adore me. girls worship me. I'm their god. why should i be afraid of adoration & worship & godliness?

And in the comments section:

floweringgarlic: gr8 questions reed. luv ur site

SoldierOfFortune: I'm not only guy traumatized

sk8erboy: ur lk a teacher reed. this is lk class only it's fun and no homework!

DirtyGirl: even tho the questions were sad they were important

greenfrog: wow it takes guys yrs 2 recover from rejection

el sexy: i'm goin 2 think abut it be4 i reject peeps from now on

The posts are amazing this time. They're much longer than usual, and there are more of them. They're thoughtful and almost . . . poignant. I really feel for these people. Some of them have been through a lot. And I'm struck again by floweringgarlic's insights. The dork of today? The hunk of tomorrow? Who *is* she?

"Wow," Ronnie says.

It's her fourth "wow." We're sitting together in front of my laptop reading everything.

"Fantastic questions, Reed," she says. "People really got into it." She scrolls up the screen. "I had no idea guys had feelings."

"Huh?" I ask. "What was that again?"

"I had no idea guys had feelings," she repeats.

I snort. "As hard as it is to accept it, Ronnie, we're human beings too."

"Sometimes I'm not so sure," she retorts.

"Don't you think I have feelings?" I ask.

"Yeah, but you're my best friend, Reed."

"I'm a guy," I say.

"And a majorly hot one," she says, kissing my cheek.

I let out a laugh. "Just because guys don't *express* their feelings doesn't mean they don't have them."

I've been reading some of my parents' books. I'm becoming a dating expert after all.

Ronnie frowns. "But Reed, guys don't seem to care."

"They care, Ronnie. They just don't show it."

"Why?"

"They're scared."

Her frown deepens. I take her hand and put it on my chest. "Hear that? I have a heart just like you do."

"I know *you* do, Reed, but . . . what about somebody like Lonnie?"

"Are you kidding? Lonnie cried for an hour after Deena dumped him yesterday."

"He did?" Her eyes are huge.

I wonder if I should've told her that. But she seems to sense I've shared something sensitive with her.

She sighs. "It's just . . . Guys call the shots."

I throw up my hands. "*Girls* call the shots, Ronnie. Girls can reject a guy every step of the way. When he asks her out. When he tries holding her hand. When he tries kissing her. When he asks her out for the second time . . ."

She pouts. "But, Reed, girls have to wait for guys to call."

"Guys have to wait for the green light for everything!" I

point to the screen. "These guys got shot down and it's years later and they're still messed up!"

I'm not happy to hear other guys went through what I did, but I *am* happy to hear I'm not the only fool on the planet.

Ronnie touches my face. "Like you?"

I nod. "Like me."

I think back to four years ago. Ronnie was extra-protective of me after what happened with Marsha. She made herself available for every school function, every party, every football game, every dance, every movie night, every pep rally, every event that year. You'd almost think we were going out if you didn't know we were just friends.

"Marsha doesn't know what she's missing," she'd say to me. "Don't worry about her, Reed, we'll show her."

And I guess we did. I don't think I appreciated what Ronnie did for me. Mostly, I was miserable over Marsha. But I appreciate it now.

Ronnie stares down at her lap.

I raise her chin. "What's the matter?"

"I'm thinking of all the guys I rejected, like, back to second grade. I feel really bad about it."

"What would make you feel better?"

"This," she says, kissing me.

. . .

Marsha Peterman drops by my locker between fifth and sixth periods a few days later.

"I didn't know, Reed," she says.

I'm not sure what she's talking about at first, but it soon becomes obvious.

"Is that . . . what I did to you?" she goes on.

I'm not sure how to answer. A girl who can squash you so badly probably wouldn't understand how much it hurt in the first place.

I start to mumble something, but Marsha says, "You . . . You've really changed the way I see things, Reed. I wanted to tell you."

She seems so sincere about it. I have trouble believing it, but maybe it's true.

I clear my throat. "I'm . . . I'm glad to hear that, Marsha."

She smiles shyly. "You're great, Reed. If you ever change your mind, let me know."

New Jersey: Where Anything Is Possible

Exit 11

"How's the contest going?" I ask Grandma after school, snatching a just-baked blondie off a plate on the counter.

"They're going to announce the winner tomorrow," she replies. "Very, very nerve-wracking."

I pause, chewing my blondie thoughtfully. "You really think a motto can change an image, Grandma?"

She studies me intently. "What do *you* think, Reed?"

I hesitate, then say, "It's a . . . starting point."

"Correct," she answers, then declares, "New Jersey: Where Grandson Geniuses Are Born and Bred."

"New Jersey," I reply with a grin, "Where Grandmothers Rock and Rule."

She laughs, and I grab another blondie and head to Ronnie's house.

It's a day after our one-month anniversary, and in that time

Ronnie and I have been inseparable. I'm *definitely* making up for lost time. I may not have kissed a girl until now, but I kiss Ronnie about eighteen times a day. I drive her to school every morning, drive her home every afternoon, hang out with her every evening, spend entire weekends with her.

The only hours I don't spend with Ronnie, in fact, are the hours I spend sleeping, but even then she's the star of some interesting dreams.

But it's still not enough for me. I want her intravenously.

I'm in love. I know it.

This is what I've been waiting for. This is what I've been searching for.

The Girlfriend Project worked big-time!

When Ronnie answers the door, I pull her into my arms. "I missed you," I whisper.

Ronnie snorts. "It's only been five minutes since we saw each other."

I bury my face in her hair. "I can't stand being away from you for even one minute."

"I think you're obsessed with me, Reed," Ronnie says, pulling back to gaze at me.

"Of course I'm obsessed with you," I reply.

She frowns slightly. "Can't you get interested in . . . collecting *Star Wars* action figures or something?"

"Nope."

She sighs. "Reed, I've been thinking about this. I worry . . ."

"What's there to worry about?" I ask, pulling her back into my arms.

She talks into my collar. "Don't you think things are getting kind of . . . intense? Living next door to each other and all?"

"That's the beauty of it, Ronnie, you're the girl next door."

She sighs into my shoulder. "Oh, Reed . . ."

"Can someone pass the barf bag?" Lonnie says, entering the room. "Some people are trying to digest around here, you know."

Ronnie smirks. "Digest in another room," she says, but she quickly disentangles herself from me.

Even after a month has gone by, I'm still struggling to navigate this whole dating-your-best-friend's-sister thing. It's become harder now that Deena's dumped Lonnie. I know he's trying to be a good sport about me and Ronnie, but I also catch him scowling at us every once in a while. I can't blame him. After all, it's almost like he's lost the two of us. I wish I had a clue how to deal with it, but I don't.

"Dude, can I talk to you?" Lonnie asks. He shoots Ronnie a look of annoyance. "Privately?"

Ronnie holds up her hands. "Hey, don't ever say I came between two guys trying to bond."

"We ain't gonna bond, we're gonna talk."

"Even better."

I follow Lonnie up to his room. He shuts the door.

"What's up?" I say, sitting uneasily on the edge of his bed.

Lonnie paces back and forth in front of me. "Look, dude, this ain't gonna be easy."

My stomach tightens. What does *that* mean? Is this the thing I've been dreading?

"I've been thinking," Lonnie says, his pacing growing more frantic. "Like, the way you used to be, your identity. Remember when we talked about identity? About image? You know, like the Jersey motto?"

I'm trying my best to follow this stream of consciousness, but I can't.

"Um," I say, "I don't think I'm . . . getting it, Lonnie. Sorry."

He looks at me with a pained expression. "Dude, you gotta understand this!" He runs his fingers through his hair distractedly. "You pretended not to want girls for four years. Right?"

"Right," I say, just to go along. I still don't know what he's getting at.

"So, I pretended to *want* girls," he says, then peers at me expectantly.

"Um," I say.

He holds out his hands. "Dude! Help me out here!"

I stammer, "You—You . . . were keeping up an image . . . of wanting girls."

"Yeah! Yeah!" he cries excitedly.

"And I was . . . keeping up an image too. But mine was the opposite of yours?"

"Yeah! Yeah!"

"So, now we're still at opposites, only the other way around?"

"Exactly," he says, punching the air.

We're both quiet for a few seconds. "So . . . ," I say.

"So I'm going to take a break for a little while."

"From . . . girls?"

"You nailed it, dude."

"Huh," I comment, which is far from brilliant, but it's something.

Lonnie looks embarrassed. "You know, Reed, I'm still not sure about you and Ronnie. But, well, you're an okay guy. No matter what happens."

"Nothing's going to happen," I say in irritation, getting up. Right?

. . .

I get an acceptance letter from Princeton that week. But there is one glitch in my perfect new life. That fuzzy orangutan Jonathan trying to steal Ronnie back from me.

See, the day after the stupid ape broke up with Ronnie, predictably, he called to say he'd changed his mind. I wanted to cheer when Ronnie hung up in his face. Come to think of it, I did cheer. Pretty loudly too.

Then the pretty, perfumed white orchids started coming, then the incredibly bad poetry—*Argh!*—take a look at this stupid stuff!

You and me,
Ronnie, Ronnie,
Prettier than a bumblebee,
Deeper than the deep blue sea,
Can't you see?
We were meant to be.
Oh, baby.

See what I mean?!

Then the champagne truffles arrived (thanks, muscle man, they were pretty good), then the ridiculous singing telegrams, then the teddy bears in pink tutus . . .

Could the guy be any more pathetically desperate?

I mean, I realize it can't be easy for him to witness the awesome spectacle of me and Ronnie engaging in nonstop liplocks at my locker, at her locker, in the school cafeteria, after school, before school. . . .

But *he* was the one who broke up with her!

Tough luck, Son of Kong.

Your loss. My gain.

Still, it totally freaked me out.

So, I almost busted a lung when, a couple of weeks later, I see Ronnie with Jonathan in an empty classroom.

I'm here to pick her up after her German class. We have study hall in the library together, and I always walk her there. But instead of waiting for me by the door like she usually does, Ronnie's still inside the classroom, and there's no one around except baboon boy, and he's standing real, real close to her.

I want to chuck him through the classroom windows, but I can't.

Why didn't I ever take karate? Kickboxing? Steroids?

The chimp chump puts a hand on Ronnie's waist.

Every drop of blood in my body goes ice-cold.

But Ronnie immediately removes Sir Hairy Gorilla's disgusting paw.

I want to give her a standing ovation. No, eighteen standing ovations!

She flounces away from him—leaving him staring after her with sad, puppy-dog eyes—and smiles when she sees me.

I take her in my arms and kiss her deeply and ferociously, but she resists me.

Jonathan slithers out of the classroom, throws me a look of bloody murder, and lumbers off.

. . .

Even a day later, my feelings of icy coldness won't go away.

"We're talking permafrost in Alaska," I tell Ronnie as we're driving to my sister's house.

"I'll warm you up later, Reed," she says, but it sounds distracted.

We're headed to Christine's place for her Tenth Annual Chocolate Extravaganza. It's a buffet party my sister gives every fall. Don't ask me how it started, why it started, what it has to do with anything, or why it's always every November. All I know is she's been doing it for ten years and nobody's complaining.

Everything on the buffet table has to be made of chocolate. *Everything*. Not just the desserts. The actual food too. Have you ever had chocolate pizza? Well, if you haven't, you haven't lived, you poor slob.

"Icier than the suds in a polar bear's Jacuzzi, Ronnie."

"I'm not going back to Jonathan, Reed."

"You promise?"

"Yes."

"Swear?"

"Yes."

"Are you willing to put it in writing?"

I'm joking. No, I'm serious.

"I would die without you, Ronnie."

"Oh, Reed," she whispers.

We're quiet the rest of the way. I can't believe I just said something so desperately, pathetically, horrifyingly clingy. I'm no better than the Ex-Ape.

When we get to my sister's, I try to act cheerful, but I'm actually miserable. Maybe I overcompensate for this by being sarcastic and annoying and offensive. For instance, when my nieces and nephews jump me at the door, as they usually do, I say, "They're like horny golden retrievers, climbing your leg and making snorting noises and stuff."

This is borderline okay. My sister laughs, and my nieces and nephews start barking playfully.

But I don't stop there. "Maybe they'll sniff people's butts one of these days. And, come to think of it, they do eat off the floor a lot and scratch themselves in inappropriate places. And the little ones do sometimes eat their you-know-what, you know, the stuff that keeps the diaper companies in business."

My sister's mortified. Ronnie pulls me down the hall into the guest bathroom and slams the door shut.

"I know you're upset, Reed," she says. "But this isn't like you. Please stop freaking out."

I gather her into my arms. "Kiss me," I say.

"Not here, Reed."

"Why not?"

"Because we're in a bathroom at your sister's house."

"So?" I lean forward and kiss her hard. She pushes me away. "Reed, quit manhandling me."

"I love you," I say.

"Oh, Reed."

"I do. I've always loved you."

She touches my face. "Reed, you're the sweetest guy in the whole world. But . . . don't you know this isn't . . . forever?"

I narrow my eyes at her. "What do you mean this isn't forever?"

She looks at me sadly. "I'm your first girlfriend, but . . . I won't be your last."

It's as if someone's splashed ice water in my face. "Yes, you will. You'll be my only one."

She sighs. "Don't you know that when you get to Princeton girls will be breaking down your door?"

"I don't want any other girls. I love you."

"Stop saying that!"

"What—are you trying to break up with me?"

Why, oh, why did I have to say it? Why did I utter the words? If only I hadn't uttered the words . . .

She bites her lip. "Reed, I've been thinking about this."

No. No. No.

"Thinking about it a lot, actually. I think, maybe, we should . . . go back to being friends. You . . . You . . . don't

need me. You could have anybody. I don't want . . . our friend-
ship to be ruined. We've been best friends for so long!"

"Ronnie, I'm sorry," I say immediately. "I won't manhandle
you anymore. I won't tell you I love you—even though I do. I
won't bring up Jonathan ever again. I won't do anything
annoying at all. I promise."

"Oh, Reed, it's not that. We're neighbors . . . We have four
years of college! This . . . wasn't a good idea."

"Well, I think it was a great idea. You're the girlfriend I've
always wanted."

"Reed, I'm the only girl you've known. That's why you like
me so much. It's almost like you . . . *imprinted* me. Like those
baby ducks you told me about, remember? But things are different for you now. I'll still be your best friend, Reed, I'll
always be your best friend."

"No."

She shakes her head. "You can't say no to this, Reed."

I get desperate. "Ronnie, please, please, don't break up
with me!"

"I'll still be your best friend!"

"But I won't be able to kiss you anymore!"

"Do you know how many girls are dying to kiss you? Why
don't you give someone else a chance?"

And, for some reason, this makes me think of Marsha sob-
bing on my shoulder when she realized she wasn't going to be
kissing me anymore.

Marsha and Ronnie have a lot in common.

They both crushed me.

I walk out of the bathroom.

And I don't stop.

. . .

I don't know why grown-ups think college is the greatest gift they can give us.

I think it stinks.

College means starting over. It means leaving home. It means not having your own room anymore. It means not seeing your best friends anymore.

It means leaving behind everything that's important.

And I'm not even going out of state.

The night of the Chocolate Extravaganza, I left my sister's house and walked all the way home. It took me two hours and I cried the whole way. I guess I forgot I had a car. When I got home, I crawled into bed, pulled the covers over my head, and stayed that way for the next two days. Good thing the next two days were Saturday and Sunday.

Mom and Dad bring my car back for me, try to lure me out of my self-imposed bed rest all weekend, bring me roast beef sandwiches and peppermint tea.

I tell them to go away.

Christine comes over with leftovers—chocolate mousse inside molded chocolate swans, chocolate casserole sprinkled with chocolate marshmallows, chocolate lasagna layered with white chocolate creme, chocolate ravioli stuffed with chocolate pudding.

I touch nothing.

Ronnie sends me five e-mails and six text-messages and calls seven times.

I ignore them all and tell my parents to tell her I'm dead.

Which I am.

Lonnie comes over four times. Each time I pretend to be sleeping.

On Sunday evening, Grandma knocks on my door. I get up and let her in. I'm still in the same clothes I wore to my sister's party. The only reason I'm allowing Grandma into my room is because I know how hard it is for her to climb the stairs. I don't want her to have made the trip for nothing.

She sits next to me on the bed and rubs my back like she used to do when I was small. "Oh, my poor, poor Reed," she says. "This is the hardest lesson of all. But everyone learns it some-time. Everything will be okay in the end. You'll see. Broken hearts heal. They do, Reed, really. You know I'd never lie to you."

I thought Marsha broke my heart when she squashed me four years ago. But that was nothing compared to this.

"I need your help, Reed," Grandma continues. "You think you could lend me a hand? I want to make a cream cake tonight. Someone I know is crazy about cream cake. I think it would cheer him up."

She kisses my cheek. "New Jersey: We May Look Tough on the Outside but We're Soft as Salt Water Taffy on the Inside. That's a good thing, Reed. Oh, I know this is the last thing you want to hear right now, but healing is growing. And growing is painful."

I follow Grandma down the stairs like an obedient puppy. As usual, she knows what's best for me. There's something about sticking your fingers into a huge bowl of whipped cream that makes you forget you're miserable.

By the time Grandma's cream cake is done, I'm feeling a tiny bit better. It's the first solid food I've consumed all weekend. I gobble up five slices all in a row.

I've never tasted anything so good.

. . .

On Monday at school, I don't bother to hide the fact that I'm crushed. I walk around with my head down all day, and go to great lengths to avoid Ronnie and Lonnie. At lunchtime, I head to the library by myself. I sit at a table in the back, unpack my school books, and stare at them. Lonnie finds me there.

"Reed, you don't have to sit here by yourself," he says quietly. "Ronnie says she'll sit at another table. You can still sit with me. Come on, I'll treat you to a nice cup of weak coffee."

"No."

"I don't like it that you're here all by yourself."

"I'd rather be here."

He sits down next to me. "I'm still your best friend, Reed," he says. "I always will be. No matter what happens."

I look at him, but say nothing.

He spends the whole period with me. He doesn't say

175

anything to me and I don't say anything to him, but I'm happy he's with me and I wish I could tell him that.

. . .

When I get home, I lie on my bed and stare at the ceiling. I'm haunted by the fact that the girl I love and need is right next door. But she might as well be on the moon.

I take out my laptop, go to www.thegirlfriendproject.com, and write a letter to my faithful fans.

> attention everyone,
> after extensive reflection, i have concluded that *The Girlfriend Project* was a miserable failure. i have also concluded that *i* am a miserable failure. sorry to disrupt your happy and productive lives with this inconvenient expression of my personal despair, but this is my site and i'll say whatever i feel like saying on it.
> love stinks,
> reed walton

It's sarcastic and painful and bitter, but I don't care. It's exactly the way I feel at the moment, and I send it on its way before I can change my mind. Then I go to the Web company that hosts the site and end my subscription.

In twenty-four hours, *The Girlfriend Project* will be history.

. . .

The rest of the week basically sucks.

Lonnie sits with me in the library at lunchtime every day. We don't talk, but I appreciate it anyway.

Ronnie tries to talk to me at least five times a day. Each time I run away from her, even though she seems upset by it.

"Reed! Please!" she always cries. "Please talk to me!"

But I don't.

On Friday, she grabs the back of my jacket as I'm hurrying off, but I wiggle out of it, leaving her holding it. Lonnie returns it to me at lunchtime.

"Love stinks," I say to him. It's the first thing I've said all week.

"Yeah," he answers.

"Why didn't you tell me?"

He gives me a sympathetic look. "I thought you knew more about it than I did. You were reading all those books, working on the site, taking all those surveys . . ."

Ha! And I had the nerve to think I was a dating expert!

"I don't know squat about it, Lonnie."

"Neither do I."

"I'm going to be a priest."

He lets out a laugh. "Nah, Reed, it won't come to that."

"I'm pretty sure it will."

"Well, if you become a priest, I will too."

We shake on it.

. . .

On Friday evening, Mom announces we're having a Family Luau Night.

My sister comes over with her family, Mom drapes us all

with pink plastic leis, and Grandma whips up pineapple boats with maraschino cherries, coconut-fried shrimp, papaya bread, and mango sorbet. My dad puts on a grass skirt for the occasion. I think he does it just to get a laugh out of me. It works.

"What do you think, Reed? Think I got a future as a tiki dancer?"

"Not a paid one," I reply.

We feast on Grandma's tropical dinner, have a hula contest, see who can say King Kamehameha ten times in a row, and watch an old Elvis Presley beach movie.

Christine sits next to me on the sofa with her arm around my shoulders, like she used to do when I was the baby brother she took care of.

My family's awesome.

. . .

On Saturday morning, I'm still in bed when Mom tells me I have a visitor. I get ready to pretend I'm sleeping, automatically assuming it's Ronnie. But when I open one eye to peek, I see Marsha Peterman standing in my doorway.

"Reed?" she whispers. "Are you . . ."

She waits a second or two, then starts to go, but I lift my head out of the covers.

"Marsha?"

She walks toward me. "Hi, Reed," she says awkwardly. "I hope . . . Were you sleeping? I didn't mean to wake you."

I sit up. "No, I wasn't sleeping."

I feel very weird. I guess Marsha does too, because she keeps glancing at her feet.

I point to a chair. "Have a seat," I say too cheerfully.

I think about hopping out of bed, getting dressed, and presenting myself as an actual human being. But I'm in a T-shirt and boxers, and I feel funny having her see me like that. So I stay in bed with the covers over me.

Marsha sits in my chair and leans toward me. "I know this is strange, Reed. I didn't know if I should come, but . . . It's just . . . I wanted to talk to you. I wanted to talk to you earlier . . . You looked so sad in school all week. And I read what you wrote on the site. . . ." She frowns. "You're not a failure, Reed. I . . . I really wanted things to work out between us. But I can see why you liked Ronnie so much. Because she was always nice to you and I . . . wasn't." She gives me a small smile. "It's my loss. Really."

My jaw falls to the floor.

She goes on. "Reed, you're gonna find someone else. I know you don't think so, but you will. And, well, the girl who gets you in the end is going to be lucky. Really, really lucky. I . . . I wanted you to know that. I wanted to tell you. That's all. That's all I wanted to say. You were so nice to me when . . . well, you know . . . I wanted to do something nice for you too."

She gets up. When I don't reply, she heads for the door.

"Marsha," I call out after her. "Thank you."

She smiles. "Hey, I heard your grandmother won the state motto contest. That's great."

"New Jersey," I say, "Where Anything Is Possible."

After Marsha leaves, I jump out of bed and get dressed. I'm going to talk to Ronnie today. I'm going to tell her she's right. We were boyfriend/girlfriend for a little more than a month. We were best friends for a little more than twelve years. Even I can see the significance of that.

But there's something I need to do first.

. . .

I park my car at the Woodrow Wilson Basketball Courts at the George Washington Municipal Park. And this time, I open my door and walk right up to her.

"Hi," I say.

"Hi," she answers. "I've been wondering when you'd finally get out of your car."

Great. She thinks I'm a stalker. Or a perv.

I take a deep breath. "Want to get a coffee somewhere? With me?"

"Yeah, I would like that a lot," she says, smiling.

I smile back. "I'm Reed, by the way."

"I know."

I cock my head to the side. "Do I know you?"

"Yeah, you do. I'm Mallory, but you might know me as . . . floweringgarlic."

Joel L. Friedman

ROBIN FRIEDMAN has worked as a children's book editor, a freelance writer, a newspaper reporter, and an advertising copywriter. She is currently a feature writer for *The Allentown Times* and lives in New Jersey with her husband, Joel, and their cats, Peppercorn, Peaches, and Butterscotch. Robin is the author of *The Silent Witness: A True Story of the Civil War* and *How I Survived My Summer Vacation: And Lived to Write the Story*. Visit her at www.robinfriedman.com.

Learn more about *The Girlfriend Project* at
www.thegirlfriendproject.com